P9-DDW-326

M   Kaminsky, Stuart M

         Rostnikov's
         vacation

MYNDERSE LIBRARY

Seneca Falls, N.Y.

ROSTNIKOV'S VACATION

By the Same Author

ROSTNIKOV'S VACATION

An Inspector
Porfiry Rostnikov Novel

STUART M. KAMINSKY

Charles Scribner's Sons
NEW YORK

Maxwell Macmillan Canada
TORONTO

Maxwell Macmillan International
NEW YORK   OXFORD   SINGAPORE   SYDNEY

Charles Scribner's Sons
Macmillan Publishing Company
866 Third Avenue
New York, NY 10022

Maxwell Macmillan Canada, Inc.
200 Eglinton Avenue East
Suite 200
Don Mills, Ontario M3C 3N1

Macmillan Publishing Company is part of the Maxwell Communication Group of Companies.

This is a work of fiction. Names, characters, places, and incidents either are the product of the author's imagination or are used fictitiously. Any resemblance to events or persons, living or dead, is entirely coincidental.

Library of Congress Cataloging-in-Publication Data
Kaminsky, Stuart M.
    Rostnikov's vacation : an Inspector Porfiry Rostnikov novel / Stuart M. Kaminsky.
        p. cm.
    ISBN 0-684-19022-2
    I. Title.
PS3561.A43R67   1991
813'.54—dc20   91-13874

10 9 8 7 6 5 4 3 2 1

Printed in the United States of America

With love for Enid, who made time begin

"Who are you?"

"A pedlar."

"How is it you know that I am being followed?"

"A friend told me."

"A spy?"

"Yes."

"And you are a spy too?"

"No," said Yevsey. But looking into Zimin's lean, pale face, he remembered the calm and dull sound of his voice, and without any effort corrected himself. "Yes, I am."

Maxim Gorky, *The Life of a Useless Man*, 1907

The KGB is a very conservative organization. It's been trained to fight international imperialism, Zionism, the Vatican, Radio Liberty, Amnesty International, Titoists, Maoists, and spying organizations. And now they are left without a job. All these bad names have disappeared from the horizon. And so they either go left, as I did, and I am not alone. But most of them go to the right. They say the country is being betrayed, the country's falling apart. They say we have to stand and fight to the end.

KGB Major General Oleg Kalugin in an address to the Congress of Communist Party Progressives in the Oktober Theater, Moscow, June 1990

ROSTNIKOV'S VACATION

PROLOGUE

The history of the secret police of Russia from the days of the czars to the present is quite convoluted, which is, perhaps, to be expected. The organization has gone through many names and many leaders.

Under the czars, the Okhrana, or the Guard, was created to protect the royal family and its staff from assassination attempts. After the Revolution, at the end of 1917, the Okhrana inspired the Cheka, or Extraordinary Commission, under Felix Dzerzhinsky, who reported directly to Lenin. After Lenin's death in 1922, the Cheka was reorganized and became the GPU, or State Political Administration. The following year, the name was changed to the OGPU, or United State Political Administration. Eleven years later, in 1934, Stalin murdered the ranking officers of the OGPU and formed the NKVD, or People's Commisariat of International Affairs. In 1941, Stalin renamed the organization NKGB, or People's Commisariat of State Security. Five years later it was renamed once more, this time the MGB, or Ministry of State Security. It wasn't until 1954, however, that the name KGB, or *Committee of State Security, was adopted. Who knows when the next change will come.*

Col. Nikolai Zhenya of the KGB knew this history well. He considered that history and his own future as he stood at the window of his office at 22 Lubyanka, the Moscow home of both KGB headquarters and the Lubyanka Prison. It was a new office into which the colonel had moved only days before, a larger office, to signify his rapid rise. The lead of the recent coat of gray paint on the walls scratched at his palate and nostrils.

To mask the taste and odor, Zhenya took a long drink from the cup of tepid tea he held in his hand. Nothing changed.

He looked around the office—new desk, new chairs, new photograph of Lenin, but a much smaller, safer photograph of Lenin, a photograph that could easily and quickly be taken down, placed in a file-cabinet drawer, and replaced with a photograph of the Kremlin at dusk. He knew there were those inside the offices around him who were considering whether they should now remove the traditional pictures of Lenin and be just a bit ahead of the other officers on the floor. Or should they wait in case the political tides so changed that their loyalty to revolutionary idealism would be admired while their carefully timed discretion would be respected? It was a game of survival, dependent not upon one's true beliefs but upon the illusion one could maintain about beliefs.

There were quiet moments like this before the day began, before the first knock at his door, when Colonel

Zhenya wondered how long he would be able to enjoy his most recent promotion.

Colonel Zhenya, who had risen rapidly through the ranks and was now, at forty-five, one of the youngest colonels in any branch of the KGB, had never truly enjoyed his successes. He had considered each betrayal, each manipulation, each intrigue in which he had engaged, a fragile rung, one as fine as a spider's thread in the ladder upward. There was no goal but to keep climbing, to keep distancing oneself farther and farther from the bottom.

The colonel, who was rapidly losing his hair and had taken to brushing it straight and severely back, pushed aside the white curtains and looked down at the traffic that swirled around the thirty-six-foot-high statue of Felix Dzerzhinsky in the square below. Dzerzhinsky had organized the Cheka—the organization that had paved the way for the KGB, "the sword of the Revolution"—for Lenin.

Now the sword of the Revolution was in the hands of the moderates, and they could not even use it to cut cheese. The sword was poised over Colonel Zhenya's head.

The colonel's office was on the top floor, and above him, since it was shortly after five in the morning, he could hear the political prisoners being exercised on the roof, their synchronized steps tramping like sheets of heavy rain.

ONE

In the evening of the very same spring day that Col. Nikolai Zhenya stood at the window of his new office in Lubyanka, three men, two in Moscow and one in Livadia, less than two miles from Yalta, were out walking.

Before the night was over, one of the men would call his wife, another would witness a murder, and the third man would be dead.

In spite of his burden, Yon Mandelstem walked briskly through the small park just beyond the Sokol Metro Station, from which he had just emerged. The case that bounced against his side was worn like a small mail sack over his shoulder. As an added precaution or to give himself better balance, he also held firmly to the cloth handle of the case.

The clouds above him closed in on the sun, and a faint sound that may have been distant thunder whispered from the west.

Mandelstem, this young, serious-looking, bespectacled man in a dark suit and equally dark tie, looked neither right nor left. He ignored the rusting twenty-foot-tall iron hammer and sickle standing just off the path beyond the trees he was passing. Nor did he even glance at the two boys fishing off the low concrete wall over the pond as he moved on.

One of the boys, a twelve-year-old named Ivan, looked over his shoulder at the blond young man who had begun to perspire from both his pace and the weight of the case and whatever was in it. Ivan thought fleetingly that the man was carrying a very small refrigerator, the kind his grandfather and grandmother had in their apartment on Pushkin Street. The shape was right, perhaps even the weight. Something tugged gently at Ivan's line. It proved to be not a fish but a ripple created by the warning wind of the coming rain. When the boy looked back, the young man with the case was gone.

Yon Mandelstem hurried on, his round spectacles slipping forward on his nose, but he did not slow his pace or loosen his grip on the case to adjust the glasses. Instead, he balanced his burden on his hip and, in annoyance, moved his hand quickly to his face to push the glasses back on his nose, knowing that they would only resume their descent until he dried the perspiration from his nose.

A distant crack of thunder and the rapidly darkening skies urged Mandelstem on even more quickly. He reached the street on the far side of the park as the rain hit. He waited for a trio of cars to pass and then tried to run. The case bounced awkwardly, uncomfortably, against his side, his hipbone catching a metallic thud with each hurried step. Reluctantly, he slowed down, resuming his rapid walk.

The two boys who had been fishing in the park ran past him, laughing at the rain. A *babushka*, an old woman wearing a black sweater and carrying a mesh bag containing what looked like some potatoes and a small block of quivering cheese, almost bumped into Yon Mandelstem on the sidewalk. Their eyes met, and through the raindrops that now dampened his vision he became alert and clutched his case to him as if he feared an attack by the soggy creature before him. She hurried away, muttering.

Yon Mandelstem was just past Building One of the four 14-floor concrete high-rise apartment buildings known to their older tenants as the Friedrich Engels Quartet when the rain abruptly stopped. It had lasted no more than a minute or two, and the sky was already clearing. A huge plane that had just taken off from the Sheremetyevo International Airport boomed overhead.

Yon Mandelstem continued, feet splashing in puddles, toward his goal, Building Two.

A few people emerged from the buildings and looked up at the clouds, which thundered a farewell and moved west, away from Moscow.

Opening the door was awkward. He could not put his case down on the wet ground, but it was difficult to open the heavy door with only one hand. Fortunately, someone came to his rescue and pushed it open.

"It stopped raining?" asked the woman who had opened the door as she stepped back to let Yon enter.

"Yes," Yon answered, removing his glasses, panting slightly.

In the dim light of the narrow hallway, Yon now recognized the woman. She was in her late thirties, possibly even forty, dark, made up, and wearing a blue dress with white flowers.

"I don't want to get my hair, my dress, wet," she said. "It's so . . . You just moved on ten? I've seen you."

"Yes," he said. There were no elevators in the Engels Quartet. In fact, there was not much to recommend the buildings or the series of slightly lower apartment buildings constructed in the 1950s and 1960s in the area. The service was terrible, worse since the reforms, for not even political pressure could get the repairmen to work. The airport was too close, and the flight patterns went directly over this section. Still, one was lucky to get an apartment, and Yon knew he would not have gotten his if he did not have special connections.

He had caught his breath, moved past the woman, and was ready to climb the stairs. He wanted to get to his room, lock the door behind him, check the treasure under his arm, and then get out of his wet clothes.

"My name is Tamara," the woman said, stepping toward him and holding out her hand.

Yon quickly tried to dry his palm on his wet trousers and held out his hand.

The woman's hand was warm and soft. She had a nice smile, a clear complexion.

"Yon Mandelstem," he said, brushing away the lock of hair that had fallen over his eyes.

"Jewish?" she said.

"Yes," he said a bit defensively, taking a quick step up the stairway.

"Not a good time to be Jewish," Tamara said, shaking her head. "Don't look so frightened. I'm not an anti-Semite. I can prove it. I'll be back in two hours. You can come to my apartment for a drink. Number eleven-six."

"I . . . I don't think."

"My husband is in Lithuania or someplace that's giving us trouble," she said with a wave of her hand, indicating either that her husband's whereabouts were of no consequence or the location of Lithuania did not matter in the course of human events.

"A soldier?" Mandelstem asked.

"No," she said with a little laugh, advancing on him. "An electrician. So?"

"So," he said, feeling the weight of the load in his aching shoulders.

"So, are you coming to my apartment later?" She was close enough for him to feel her breath on his face. It was warm, a bit sweet.

"Perhaps," he said, turning suddenly and starting up the stairs. "Perhaps another time."

"Won't be another time," she said, shaking her head. "I'm using the apartment of a friend. She's coming back in a few days and I'll have to go. Tonight will be best."

"I'll . . ." Yon began.

"Think about it," she said, giving him a broad smile and turning her back as she headed for the door.

Yon began to climb the stairs.

Below him, Tamara shook her head, touched her

breasts with both hands to be sure they were still there, and went into the evening, almost bumping into a lean man wearing a workman's jacket and a cap pulled down over his eyes.

"*Prastee't'e,* excuse me," she said with a smile that showed even white, though a bit large, teeth, of which she was particularly proud. The man did not look at her.

Yon Mandelstem was exhausted when he reached the door to his apartment. He put down his case, glancing around the empty corridor to be sure no one was watching. No doors were cracked open. A sound that may have been bitter laughter came from one of the apartments nearby, but he could not tell which one. He got his key out, opened the door, placed his case inside, stepped in, turned on the light, and closed the door behind him.

He looked around the small room, locked the door, took off his glasses, placed them in his jacket pocket, and moved the case across the room to the desk in the corner before he began to strip off his wet clothes. He threw the clothes in the general direction of the worn but serviceable dark sofa against the wall.

Then, naked except for his sox, he moved into the second small room, which served as a bedroom. He reached over and took off his sox as he hopped toward the little cubbyhole in which a shower beckoned.

He threw back the shower door and found himself facing a grinning man with bad teeth.

There was a chill in the Crimean evening air. Georgi Vasilievich pulled up the collar of his jacket, shook his

shoulders, and began walking along the czar's lane from
Livadia to Oreanda. Although it was still early in the
evening, the thick woods blocked out the setting sun,
making it seem much later.

Vasilievich walked slowly. He told himself it was
because he enjoyed the woods, the outdoors. He was a
man of the city, and he wished to savor the clean air,
the solitude. He told himself these things, but something inside him would not listen. Georgi Vasilievich
was a policeman, a good policeman, who recognized a
lie even when it was one he was telling to himself. No,
the truth was that he was getting old. He was tired.
Perhaps General Petrovich was right to insist that he
take his vacation, that he spend several weeks in the
sanitarium for rest and therapy. He had been working
hard, as had all in the GRU, the chief intelligence directorate of the Soviet General Military Staff. Unrest in
the military was evident at all levels. The work load
was impossible. And it was being conducted with no
reward, no appreciation from the people, no appreciation from their superiors, who were too distracted in
the new turmoil created by Gorbachev to reward with
even a word the efforts of . . .

The path turned and brought him to the rotunda at
the seashore. He always stopped at the rotunda. In the
week he had been making this trip since Dr. Vostov
had prescribed the walk, Vasilievich had paused at the
rotunda, both coming and going, to admire the view
and to catch his breath.

Vasilievich had a heart condition. One could not
argue with that fact. He had experienced a heart attack.
But it was four years earlier, and his health reports had

been well within the bounds of acceptability from the
moment he had been released from the hospital. The
rest would, he had reluctantly concluded, be good for
him. But, fortunately, in Yalta he had found more than
the sight of the sea and woods to occupy him. He had
discovered a puzzle that he believed he had now solved.

Georgi Vasilievich put his large arthritic hands on
the railing and looked out at Machtovaya Rock, its gray
bulk split in two. He had been told by an old woman
who helped clean the sanitarium that archaeologists had
found a cave beneath the rocks, under the water level,
where ancient ancestors of man once dwelt.

An animal or another late walker stirred leaves on
the path behind him. Vasilievich did not turn. He
imagined or tried to imagine for a breath of a moment
that it was his wife, Magda, a few steps behind him,
that she would join him to look where his eyes now
turned, at the Krestovy Cliff, the bloody cliff where,
Vasilievich knew, the White Guards had shot the revolutionary sailors and workers of both Sebastapol and
Yalta. At the base of the cliff stood the church that had
been built on the ruins of a palace destroyed by fire
more than one hundred years ago. He needed no old
woman to tell him that. The church stood only a few
hundred yards from the sanitarium, whose roof now
caught the last rays of the sun.

Magda had died five, no, nine years earlier, he
thought. It couldn't be. But it was. He smiled. Senti-
ment. He was not a sentimental man. He had displayed
no great affection for Magda while she lived. In fact,
they had fought often, and he could recall no instance
of their having embraced over the final twenty years,

and yet he missed her. When she died, he had secretly rejoiced, his somber eyes downcast, the suggestion of tears threatening. He rejoiced in his freedom. He could work whatever hours he wished, smoke his pipe in his underwear, watch the television. But that sense of freedom survived less than a year. He was not sure how much less. The feeling of loss had come gradually.

This time the sound on the path behind him made Vasilievich turn. He should be wearing his glasses. He knew that, but Georgi was a proud man. He had once been a large man, but the years, his illness, and something in the soul that he could not quite understand and in which he did not believe had begun to shrink him.

There was nothing, no one, there. But still, it did not hurt to be cautious. He bent down at the edge of the rotunda and pretended to tie his shoe while he glanced toward the trees without turning his head.

Vasilievich resumed his journey and became absorbed almost immediately in the problem he had been picking at for the past few days, the problem he had been reluctant to share with Rostnikov, who would have been sympathetic but have thought him an old fool.

Vasilievich would have liked to quicken his step, but he hesitated, fearing that sudden jolt, the loss of breath he had experienced but once four years ago before his heart attack.

"I am better," he said to himself, moving forward, head down, as if against a strong, chill wind.

"I am fine," he said aloud but not loudly.

And with that his decision was made. He wanted no

more of this place, this solitude. He would go back to the sanitarium, pack his things, and inform Dr. Vostov that he would be returning to Moscow on the first available plane. He had an open ticket. He need but call the air—

Definitely something behind him. Definitely. He stopped and stepped off the path next to a tree. He was, himself, thin, gnarled. From a distance he could have been a branch growing from the base of a dark tree. He slowly, carefully, removed his glasses from his jacket pocket and placed them on the end of his nose. When they were properly perched, Georgi Vasilievich stood motionless, as he had done hundreds of times in the past while stalking a criminal. He willed his breathing to be shallow, to mingle with the sounds of the woods, the waves brushing the shore beyond the trees. He had no weapon. Why would anyone need a weapon on a hospital vacation? His pistol was locked in the metal box in his office desk in Moscow.

He stood listening for five or ten minutes. Nothing. Rostnikov was right, or would have been right if Vasilievich had been foolish enough to share his idea with him. All he had told Rostnikov was that he was working on something, putting notes together that he might soon share with him, but he was not prepared to do so yet. Georgi Vasilievich was an old fool who had played too many games, seen too many deaths. Georgi had looked over at Rostnikov with the knowing little smile he had cultivated for more than forty years, a smile that told suspect and colleague alike that he, Vasilievich, knew something, had a secret of great importance to this suspect or colleague.

He stepped back onto the path, feeling even more chilled. The blood circulated poorly in his feet, and his hands were numb.

"It's not cold," he hissed to himself, chiding himself silently as he walked. "You're an old fool talking to himself, an old fool who can't think straight, can't tell—"

Two men stood before him on the path. He sensed them long before he saw them and looked up. He could not run or hide. His body would no longer tolerate or support such action. He assessed the situation quickly, efficiently, and walked toward the men whose faces he could not yet see. When he was perhaps two yards from them, he stopped, pushed his glasses up and found that he could make out their faces, could see what they were wearing. One man was a mountain, massive, wearing a blue sweater and a dark frown. The second man was small, very small, and thin, with a wild eye that did not join its partner in looking at Georgi Vasilievich.

And in that moment all became clear. He had not imagined it. He had figured it out, had figured it all out. He fleetingly wished that he had shared his knowledge with Porfiry Petrovich Rostnikov. He stopped walking as a large wave beyond the trees slapped the shore.

Though the film at the Oktober Theater was not over and Emil Karpo had never seen it, indeed, had not been in a movie theater for more than twenty-five years, he stood up and left. He had been sitting in a seat on the aisle while above him on the screen fat Hungarians were laughing, acting like buffoons, and chasing thin blond women who occasionally spoke words in French.

Emil Karpo did not dislike movies. But neither did he like them. He followed the young woman who had left the vast auditorium of 2,500 seats moments before. Lenin had said that film had a function, a crucial propagandistic function. Movies were supposed to have brought enlightenment, reinforcement of revolutionary ideas, and idealism. Generally, Karpo considered both movies and television pointless narcotics. Lenin had praised film, and Karpo had taken it as an act of faith, which he called reason, that Lenin knew what he was talking about. Perhaps at one time films did have some seductive power that could be used to ease the people into the Revolution, but that was long ago. Perhaps the words of Lenin had great power to convince those who wished to truly believe, but that was not so long ago. Now statues of Lenin were being toppled in provincial towns. The slowly growing truth of the dream was being ignored, and on twenty-foot-high screens in the darkness Hungarians and Americans were showing their teeth and selling illusions.

However, in this case, the darkness and relative quiet of the theater was a distinct improvement over the basement den, the Billy Joel, where the young woman he was following had just spent two hours in smoke-filled and drug-dimmed purple light, listening to some band called *Pe'r'ets*—Pepper—scream and blast something called heavy metal on their electronic instruments.

Emil Karpo had not dared enter. He was at least twenty years older than the youngest patron in the Billy Joel, and he knew that there was no way he could sit

inconspicuously. Emil Karpo was a tall, corpselike figure with vaguely Oriental features. His hair was dark
and thinning, his cheekbones high, his skin tight and
pale, and his face expressionless. All of Emil Karpo's
clothing was black, even his T-shirts and several turtle-
necks. He was known among criminals and police alike
as the Tartar or the Vampire. He knew this and did
not mind. He also knew from the faces of those he
encountered that they sensed a cold, silent fury that he
in fact did not feel.

And so he knew he could not enter the Billy Joel.
Instead, he had found a dirty window in an alleyway
behind the club and had used his two-inch-long glass
cutter to make a hole so small that it would probably
not be noticed till someone came to clean the window,
if that ever happened.

He had watched her through the hole, had watched
the others, had seen drugs passed, bodies sold. Somewhere within him he was ill. It was not so much that
these young people were corrupted but that after seventy years of Soviet rule there was more chaos than
there had been since the czars. The club had been
chaos, noise, decay. Had he entered, he knew he would
be enduring one of his headaches within minutes. So
he had watched from the window, patiently. Had
watched as he had so many times in the past.

The beautiful, restless young woman had consumed
four drinks and with withering looks and hissed words
of acid had disposed of two young men and one young
woman who made advances to her as she sat alone at a
table commanding an unobstructed view of the madmen
screaming on the platform. Her name was Carla. That

was one of the facts about her that Emil Karpo had entered in ink in his pocket notebook. This information and whatever he discovered this day would be transferred to thicker lined notebooks when Karpo got back to his apartment.

Carla spent most of her time staring at her drink. She appeared to pay little attention to the band that blared not five yards from where she sat. Suddenly, in the middle of a song about hatred of cowardly parents screamed by a woman-child with orange hair, Carla got up and strode out.

She had signaled for a cab in front of the café. She had no difficulty getting one. Taxis stopped for beautiful girls. And this beautiful girl was dressed in a very tight-fitting red dress with a three-inch black belt of patent leather. Her thick red hair, which matched the dress, tumbled wildly down her back and over her shoulders.

Cabs also stopped for Emil Karpo, as one did now, when he stepped into the street and held up his hand, but it stopped for quite different reasons than did the cab that picked up Carla. The woman who drove the cab that Karpo stopped was named Sophie Mirbat, who had been driving for the past ten hours and was on her way in for the night. She had accepted Karpo's statement that he was a policeman, had given her name when he asked for it, and had followed the other cab dutifully in the hope that it would come to a stop soon so she could rid herself of the Vampire behind her and get home to her father and son before midnight. But it was not to be.

When they pulled up to the Oktober Theater on Kalinin Prospekt, the Vampire had said, "You will wait here for me, Sophie Mirbat. You will wait even if it is till dawn."

Sophie Mirbat considered and abandoned the idea of simply driving away when the man went into the theater. This was not a man to disappoint. Instead, she looked up at the mosaic mural on the facade of the theater, the movie-frame-like depictions of historical events in Soviet history, the storming of the Winter Palace, the Civil War. She sat quietly looking up at the mural as she wondered whether she dared charge the man for the time she was going to put in.

Now, less than an hour later, the beautiful woman Karpo was following made a phone call from the booth next to the theater. Karpo was careful to stay back in the shadows. He had learned that those who saw him did not forget him, but he had also learned how to remain unseen.

From where she was parked, the cabdriver, Sophie Mirbat, could see both Karpo and the young woman he was watching. She considered starting her engine but decided to wait. Gas was dear and going up in price.

Carla's call took a few seconds. She did all the talking and then hung up in anger, her eyes meeting the disapproving glance of a passing old couple. She stared at the couple defiantly with one hand on her hip and the other with her thumb hooked into her black belt. The old couple moved on. That she was beautiful was without question, but her beauty was not an issue with which Karpo cared to concern himself. He had lived his adult life with dedication to the Revolution, had lived only to cleanse the state, bring about the world ideal for which Lenin died and in which Karpo believed. That he had a body, had needs, emotions, he acknowledged. He did not find joy in this acknowledgment, but he well knew that man was an animal and as an animal he had needs. It was better, he had long ago concluded, to meet these needs, compartmentalize them.

Karpo needed his work. There was nothing else. There was not meant to be anything else. His small fifth-floor apartment was dedicated to his work and contained only a narrow bed, a small chest of drawers, a rough wooden desk, and shelves filled with black-bound notebooks in which were details of every case Karpo had worked on in addition to hundreds of unclosed files, unsolved cases on which he worked in his evenings and on his days off. But he was being overwhelmed. Crime was no longer a dot here and a dot there, dots that might be connected to form a pattern of corruption that could be eliminated line by line with patience. No, crime in Moscow was now a giant splatter of blue paint.

Emil Karpo's hope of salvation lay in his total immersion in his work, and the case on which he was now working was quite therapeutic.

He had, he told Colonel Snitkonoy the day before, a lead on the young man who was suspected of killing a German businessman named Bittermunder near the Moscow River a week earlier. An informant had told him that a young woman with red hair named Carla, a regular at a new rock café called the Billy Joel on Gorky Street, had been talking about the crazy boy she was living with, a boy who had killed a German.

So when Colonel Snitkonoy had ordered him to take a vacation and get out of Moscow, Emil Karpo had disobeyed. The idea of a week away from Moscow, when he might be so close to a murderer, brought on the threat of one of his headaches. The reasons for Karpo to take a vacation now were quite reasonable. Rostnikov was gone. They had been working on a number of investigations together, so it would make sense to put them aside until they were both present. Karpo had argued that he had taken off a great deal of time for surgery and recovery. His right arm had been damaged first during pursuit of a burglar and later in an explosion in Red Square, where he had confronted a terrorist and for which he had received a Moscow Medal. That time off, said Colonel Snitkonoy, was in the line of duty, not a merited vacation.

Normally, Karpo accepted his vacations willingly. They gave him time to work on his unsolved cases, but this was the first time he had been ordered out of the city, and it came at a time when he was in great need of his work.

"If I allow you to remain," the Gray Wolfhound had said, "you will continue to work. Go, renew your vitality. I have a small dacha near Borodino. Or visit your relatives in Kiev. Read. Sleep. Look at the trees. Come back refreshed. There is much to do, and we need your full and healthy attention."

It would have been useless for Karpo to say more, and he could not and would not explain. And so he was soon to be officially on vacation. Officially, he informed the colonel's assistant, Pankov, that in a few days, after he cleared up some minor items, he would be off with relatives on a farm near Kiev that had no phone.

Unofficially, he stood in the shadows of the outer lobby of the Oktober Theater and watched a beautiful girl who might steer him to the leader of a gang that may have been involved in the murder of a German businessman. He had no intention of leaving Moscow until he succeeded in this task.

Carla had time to smoke one cigarette and pace back and forth twenty-two times before a car pulled up in front of the theater, a late-model Chaika, well cared for, catching the lights of the theater and the street. A man got out of the car, a man with neatly cut dark hair and a short, well-trimmed black beard flecked with gray. The man looked around in all directions as the woman climbed into the car and closed the door.

Cars went by on the street, but still the man did not get back into the car. He continued to look in all directions, even into the lobby of the Oktober, directly at the tall man in black who was deep within the shadows.

"Come on," Carla called impatiently to the bearded man, whose hand rested on the door of the car.

"Adnoo' meenoo'too," he said calmly. "Wait a minute."

Even at this distance, Karpo thought he detected an accent.

The woman, clearly irritated, said, "The movie was terrible."

The man said nothing, continuing to scan the street, the doorways.

The woman rolled her window closed, and after a beat, the bearded man, now satisfied, opened his door, got in the car, and drove away.

Karpo strode quickly to the street. The car with the bearded man and the woman was moving to his right. He did not look to his left, where the headlights of Sophie Mirbat's cab suddenly came on. His eyes were still following the disappearing Chaika when the cab pulled up to the curb. He reached down, opened the door, and got into the front seat.

"There," Karpo said, pointing in the direction of many dots of light from many cars. "That car."

"Where?" asked Sophie, moving back into traffic.

"Drive," said Karpo.

"I'm driving," she said. "But . . ."

"Faster, around."

"I don't see it," said Sophie Mirbat.

"I see it," said Karpo. "Go more slowly. Don't get too close."

"To what? Where are we going?" she began, and looked at Karpo. The look she got in return convinced her that it would be best to say no more.

Karpo believed they were not going far but that it might take them a long time to get there. He believed they were not going far because the car the woman had called had come quickly from where she had summoned it. He believed it might take long because the bearded driver was being cautious, very cautious. It would be a game. The bearded man would drive as if he were being followed even though he probably did not believe that he was being followed. He would watch, drive around side streets, and take Carla where she was going only after he was sure he was not being followed.

And so they drove. In circles the Chaika and the cab drove. Down the same streets and past the same corners

they drove. Sophie Mirbat said nothing, simply followed the directions given by the ghostly man at her
side. Twenty minutes later the Chaika arrived at a point
they could have reached in five minutes.

"They're not worried about the cost of petrol," Sophie
Mirbat said, and regretted it almost immediately.

"Stop here," said Karpo.

She stopped. They were on a side street just off Smolenskaya Square, near the Borodinsky Bridge. Beyond
the tall buildings, less than a block away, was the Moscow River. Karpo got out of the car. A boat horn
bleated in the night.

"You want me to . . . ?" Sophie Mirbat whispered,
rolling down the window.

"Go," said Karpo, handing her some bills.

Sophie needed no further orders, and she did not
pause to count the money. She made a U-turn and
rolled back into darkness.

The beautiful woman with red hair got out of the car
almost a block away and slammed the door behind her
in anger. The bearded man drove off slowly, and Emil
Karpo moved down the street in their direction. The
woman entered an apartment building, took out a key,
and opened the inner wooden door.

Karpo found a dark door, a closed shop, and stood
back, watching the windows of the apartment building.
His eyes did not blink. They took in the facade, and
then a light went on in one of the darkened windows
six floors above. He turned his head toward the light,
counted the floors without looking at them, decided
which apartment she had entered, and then stood erect,
determined, no matter how long he would have to stand

here, no matter how many nights, not to think until the moment came to act.

He did not have long to wait.

Slightly less than five minutes after he arrived in front of the building near Smolenskaya Square, the window he was watching exploded, showering the dark street with glass and releasing a blast of screaming music. Above the blare came a choking cry as Carla plummeted naked toward the street, her red hair billowing out, catching the light from the broken window behind her.

Karpo could see her frightened face as she fell. For an instant he was even sure that her eyes made contact with his, pleading for help he could not give. And then her knee hit a parked car, her hands reached out to grab something, to stop what could not be stopped. Her breasts quivered as she spun over completely like an awkward gymnast. Then she struck the street and was no longer beautiful or alive.

Karpo looked up at the shattered window as he stepped into the street. Framed by jagged edges of glass, backed by the blasting voice of a woman singing something in English and the sound of a screeching electric guitar, stood a figure in dark leather, a grinning figure with a spike growing out of its head.

TWO

Porfiry Petrovich Rostnikov was tired. He had, for the first time in twenty years, done nothing for eight days, and each day he had grown more weary as he fell into a routine. Up at seven, bread, coffee with Sarah, if she was up, a stroll to the beach, if his leg was not too stiff from the sea air, and several hours of watching those bathers who were willing to ignore the warnings about possible pollution in the Black Sea. On the beach, when he was not watching the bathers, he read one of the seven books he had brought with him from Moscow and paid unconscious attention to any warnings or demands his left leg might issue.

Rostnikov's leg was not to be trusted. It had been injured when Rostnikov, a fifteen-year-old boy fighting the Germans outside of Rostov, had encountered a tank, which he succeeded in destroying. He had come back from the war, become a policeman, married, and had a son whom, in a moment of long-regretted zeal, he and his wife had named Iosef, in honor of Stalin. He had worked his way into the Procurator General's Office, only to be transferred on "temporary but open-ended duty" at the age of fifty-five to the MVD—the police, uniformed and ununiformed, who direct traffic, face the public, maintain order, and are the front line of defense against crime. It had been a clear demotion for his too-frequent clashes with the Komitet Gosudarstvennoi Besopasnosti, the State Security Agency, the KGB, clashes that were inevitable because the KGB had the power to investigate any crime that posed a threat to national security or the economy and the KGB interpreted its powers broadly.

For more than a year, Rostnikov and his closest associates had been on the staff of Colonel Snitkonoy, the Gray Wolfhound. The responsibilities of the colonel's staff were largely ceremonial, but boundaries between the branches were so thinly drawn that ceremony frequently became substance if an individual investigator so desired.

After watching the bathers and reading for a half hour or so—he was almost through a John Lutz novel about a woman in New York who takes in a murderous roommate—Rostnikov would rise, get the circulation going again in his leg, and then read some more. He had discovered a pattern among the bathers at the crowded, rocky beach. Early morning belonged to the serious bathers, who sought the invigorating confrontation of the cold Black Sea water. Theirs was a ritual to be taken seriously, and they certainly did not look as if they enjoyed themselves.

Then came the short-time vacationers and families, who felt obligated to bring their blankets down and join the crowds on the long, narrow shale beaches. Few of them stayed in the water long. They wanted only to say that they had entered and enjoyed the sea. Many of them were fat. Rostnikov himself, known to colleagues as "the Washtub," was solid and compact and heavy, the legacy of his parents and the leg that allowed him little movement. But his devotion to lifting weights had kept him from looking like the nearby vacationers, who seemed not in the least embarrassed to show their bellies over brief swimsuits.

In the very late afternoon and early evening, when the sun was no longer high and after Rostnikov was gone, the beach would belong to younger bodies, and occasionally there would be real laughter. Rostnikov had planned to spend more time with his wife on the beach in the early evening, but Sarah, who was still recovering from rather delicate brain surgery, did not yet have the energy for a late-day excursion after her necessary afternoon visits to the Oreanda sanitarium.

Just before noon each day, Rostnikov would take the slow walk back for a modest lunch with Sarah at the Lermontov Hotel, after which they would take the short bus ride to the sanitarium, where Sarah would receive her treatments while Rostnikov used the weights in the small physical therapy room. Then back to the hotel, where the attentive Anton, one of the hotel waiters who had taken them under his wing, would stop by to ask if they had a good day or needed anything.

Following a brief or lengthy rest, depending on which Sarah needed, they would eat in the dining room at their usual table, and Rostnikov would practice his English on the American tourists, most of whom grumbled about the poor accommodations, the poor service, and the pollution of the sea and who only reluctantly admitted to an appreciation of the area's beauty. And then, about an hour or two before sunset, as Sarah and Rostnikov sat on their wooden folding chairs, looking out at the sea from the ridge next to the Lermontov Hotel, Georgi Vasilievich would show up, gaunt, slow, sadly smiling.

Rostnikov and Sarah had encountered Vasilievich at the sanitarium on their first day in Yalta. Rostnikov and Vasilievich had met each other many times over the years when Rostnikov was an inspector with the Procurator General's Office and Vasilievich a senior investigator in the intelligence directorate. Vasilievich had, in his younger days, served undercover in USSR embassies in Paris, Bangkok, and Istanbul. By 1972, he had returned for permanent duty inside the Soviet Union on assignments related to possible foreign agents operating in Moscow. Since Rostnikov's demotion to MVD ceremonial staff, he had not run into Vasilievich, and at first he had not recognized the obviously ill man in the corridor, but Vasilievich had recognized him.

"Porfiry Petrovich," he had said, shaking his head and holding out his hand American style. They had never been intimate, had never been close enough for a friendly hug, though Porfiry Petrovich had felt the urge when he finally recognized the man who had in the few years since he had last seen him moved uncomfortably into old age. "What's wrong? Why are you here? The old leg wound?"

"No," Porfiry Petrovich had said, not wanting to explain, to open a dialogue with Vasilievich, who was a notorious busybody. He was also, Rostnikov knew, one of the most tenacious and valued investigators in the GRU.

"It's me," Sarah had said. "I had an operation. Brain growth."

A look of pain had crossed Vasilievich's face; whether from Sarah's news or his own malady was not clear.

"I'm fine now," Sarah had said. That was not quite true, Rostnikov had thought. Her red hair had grown back, but she had lost weight, weight she had trouble regaining, and her cheeks were not as pink as before, though he hoped the Yalta sun would help.

"My wife died a few years ago," Vasilievich had said, looking beyond them as if he could see her ghost.

"I'm sorry," Sarah had said.

Vasilievich had shrugged.

"I'm here because I was ordered to come," he had said, with an enormous resigned sigh. "Order directly from General Pluskat. Heart checkup. Emphysema. Fifty years of smoking, but I feel no worse than I have for a decade, and, Porfiry Petrovich, I tell you I am bored here. I need my work, not memories and regrets."

Porfiry Petrovich had politely invited Georgi Vasilievich to visit them at the hotel. Neither Sarah nor he had expected Vasilievich to come, and Rostnikov had secretly hoped he would not accept the invitation, for Vasilievich was walking gloom and horror stories.

But since that first encounter in the corridor of the sanitarium, Vasilievich had made the slow and tortured journey each night to the Lermontov Hotel to watch the setting sun, drink tea, and talk. And, much to his surprise, Rostnikov had found himself anticipating these visits and even enjoying Georgi Vasilievich's company. The talk had been of the past, not the personal past but the professional past, the murders, thefts, their encounters, particularly the Fox-Wolfort investigation in 1971 in which a visiting East German major, who may have been a West German agent, had been found dead in a broom closet of the memorial chapel of the Grenadiers, directly behind KGB headquarters on Dzerzhinsky Square. The German had been skewered with a Byzantine cross ripped from the wall. Vasilievich and Rostnikov had cooperated in finding the prostitute who had done it when the German had attempted to rape her in the broom closet.

Rostnikov had not sought this vacation. In fact, he had fought against it. Too much was going on in Moscow. Citizens had just voted in the first open national election since the Bolsheviks had been soundly beaten in 1917. The Party Congress was coming up. People were going mad on the right and left. Young people were ignoring the law. Jews, even one of Sarah's cousins, Rafael the carpenter, were being singled out, beaten, blamed for the economic change. The lines in stores were longer than they had been since after the war, and the assumed loss of cultural identity was erupting among even the lesser-numbered minorities. There was not less crime but more since the reforms, far more and far more violent. There was no foundation. The law and those who enforced it were no longer a strong kiln but a leaking sieve punctured by the three-pronged pitchfork of *perestroika* (economic restructuring), *glasnost* (openness), and *demokratizatsiya* (democratization). Growing pains, Sarah had suggested, and he had agreed, but he thought it best to be present and in Moscow during the growth.

"But," the Gray Wolfhound, Colonel Snitkonoy, had said, standing before Rostnikov in his office in Petrovka, the central police building, "your presence will not change all this. It will be waiting for you when you return."

The Wolfhound had spoken with his usual great confidence. He was a man buoyed by recent victory. Chance, Rostnikov, and his own instinct for survival had strengthened his political position over the past several months. Colonel Snitkonoy was a tall, slender man with a magnificent mane of silver hair. His brown uniform was always perfectly pressed. His three ribbons of honor, neatly aligned on his chest, were just right in color and number. On formal occasions and for appropriate foreign visitors, whom he frequently escorted, the colonel could trot out an array of medals with the brightness of a small star and the weight of an immodest planet. He had been, at the moment he ordered Rostnikov on vacation, impressive as he strode, hands clasped behind his back.

When he had first been transferred to the Wolfhound's command, Rostnikov had taken the man for a fool, and perhaps the colonel was a fool of sorts, but he was a fool with a sense of survival, a fool who rewarded loyalty and appreciated it, a fool who was no fool at all.

Rostnikov had begun to speak in protest that morning less than two weeks before, but the colonel had raised his right hand to stop him.

"Your wife could benefit from the sanitaria, the sea water," he said. "How many sanitaria are there in Yalta?"

The only other person in the room was the Wolfhound's assistant, Pankov, who correctly assumed the question was for him.

"Forty or—" Pankov began, and was interrupted by the Wolfhound.

"Yalta is the Venice of the Soviet Union," the Wolfhound had whispered, as if it were a secret to be shared only by the three men in the room. Rostnikov did not respond. Pankov nodded in agreement.

Pankov, a near dwarf of a man who was widely believed to hold his job because he made such a perfect contrast to the colonel, was a perspirer, a rumpled bumbler whose few remaining strands of rapidly graying hair refused to obey grease or brush.

"Gorky lived in Yalta. Chekhov, too," the Wolfhound had said.

Rostnikov, of course, knew this but said nothing. Pankov had looked mildly surprised at this information.

"You can visit his house, the house where Chekhov wrote *The Three Sisters, The Cherry Orchard*," the Wolfhound went on. "Pankov will make the arrangements for everything. This is an order."

And so it was. And so Porfiry Petrovich Rostnikov had found himself standing on the hill on which the Lermontov Hotel was built, folding chair under one arm, American paperback under the other, feeling more tired than he had after many a long night of interrogating a murderer or waiting in a car for the appearance of a car thief or burglar.

* * *

From the moment of their arrival and from nowhere and everywhere the waiter Anton had appeared. Anton seemed to be from another time, another planet. Apparently he did not understand that Soviet waiters and hotel personnel did not cater to the needs of their customers. The Soviet way was to be wary, to wait to be asked and then to treat any request as an imposition. Anton, however, was not in the least bit surly. He had, he said, lived his entire life, except for his military duty, in Yalta. He, and his father before him, had been named for Anton Chekhov, and both had attended School Number 5, which had previously been the Yalta Gymnasium for Girls, the gymnasium, Anton said proudly, where the great Chekhov had been on the board of trustees.

"My grandfather was a waiter in this hotel, as was my father. My grandfather had the honor of serving Chekhov himself on many occasions. Chekhov was very fond of fish. Would you like some help with your chair, Comrade Rostnikov?" he asked with a very small smile that showed reasonably even though not large teeth.

Anton was a short man with wire-rim glasses and short brown hair. He was, at best, wiry; at worst, scrawny.

"I'm fine, Anton," said Rostnikov.

"Back for lunch at one?" Anton asked as Rostnikov started down the slope for another morning at the beach while Sarah rested.

"At one," Rostnikov agreed.

"Drinks?" asked Anton, whose voice was a bit farther

away as Rostnikov came to the bottom of the slope. He
was sure Anton's hands were clasped together.

"Ask Mrs. Rostnikov when she gets up," Rostnikov
called over his shoulder.

The sky threatened rain, but Rostnikov trudged on.
Families hurried past him toward the beach, their beach
shoes clapping on the path. Rostnikov limped resolutely, folding chair under his arm, anxious to finish his
book. Ten minutes later, he positioned himself in more
or less his usual spot and was pleased to see a reasonably handsome woman in a red swimsuit lying on a
blanket not more than twenty yards away. Thunder
rumbled, but the clouds were not dark enough to clear
the beach or make Rostnikov think of an early return.
Sarah would be sleeping, resting. If it rained, it would
rain, and he would get wet as he walked to one of the
cafés near the beach, where he could eat an English
biscuit and continue reading while having an overpriced
cup of coffee or tea.

He was comfortable in his chair, absorbed in his
book, letting conversation and the general wave of water
and voices wash around him when a single word caught
his attention.

"Vasilievich," came a man's voice.

Rostnikov looked up. A man nearby, a bony old man
with a little gray beard and a potbelly, had said the word
to a lumpy woman sitting beside him on a blanket.

Rostnikov rose, his leg already a bit stiff, tucked the
book under his arm, and moved to the bony man.

"Pardon me," he said. "What did you say about Vasilievich? Who . . . ?"

"*Yah n'e poneema'yoo vahs,*" the man said slowly. "I

don't understand. We are Hungarians. *Gavaree't'e pazha-ha'lsta, me'dlenn'eye.* Please speak a little more slowly."

"You speak English?"

"A little," the bony man said.

"Vasilievich. You said something about someone named Vasilievich," Rostnikov said in English.

"Correct," the man said. The woman next to the man turned and shaded her eyes with her right hand to look up at Rostnikov. "Someone with the name Vasilievich in another room in the hall from my wife's father at the sanitarium. He died during the night. Not her father. Vasilievich."

"Georgi Vasilievich?"

"Yes," said the bony man. "You know . . . knew him? They said it was heart. Man had a bad heart. Died in a chair outside the sanitarium. Must have been there a long time. Found by a Mrs. Yemelova."

"Yemelyanova," the woman corrected him.

"Yes, correct," said the bony man. "She found him. You knew him?"

"Yes," said Rostnikov. "Thank you."

Rostnikov broke his routine. He returned to the hotel, informed Sarah of Vasilievich's death, and with Sarah went down to the lobby to call the local MVD office. He identified himself to the woman who answered, and she confirmed that Georgi Vasilievich was dead and that his body lay in the Dysanskay Sanitarium.

Anton appeared. "You're back early," he said. "I saw you come back. Is everything well? Do you want early lunch?"

The Lermontov lobby was small, dark, and, at this hour, almost empty except for a trio huddled in conversation around a small table near the window, the clerk behind the desk, and an odd duo—a huge, formidable-looking bear of a man and a small, nervous man with a dancing eye—in a far corner. The man with the dancing eye seemed to be looking at Rostnikov.

"Would you like early lunch?" Anton repeated.

Rostnikov did not answer.

"What is being served?" Sarah asked.

"Sour cabbage in vinegar and oil, veal loaf, and sugared apples."

"No, thank you," said Sarah.

Anton looked as if he were about to try again, but Rostnikov's vacant look stopped him.

"We'll go to the clinic early today," Rostnikov said softly.

"Yes," said Sarah, taking his arm. She looked at the mildly bewildered Anton and said, "Someone my husband knew for many years died."

Anton nodded.

Sarah looked pale. It was not that she or Porfiry Petrovich had any great affection for Vasilievich. Rostnikov knew that Vasilievich was not an easy man to like, and Sarah had been careful to say that Vasilievich was not a friend, but "someone my husband knew." Nonetheless, Vasilievich had been with them, alive the day before, and her recent operation reminded her that life was fragile and death always nearby.

"I'll get my things," Sarah said.

"A sandwich to take with you?" Anton offered. "Or a *vobla*, a dried fish, to nibble on the way?"

"Are you like this with everyone?" asked Rostnikov.

"Like what?" Anton asked, mopping up crumbs with his hand from a small white wooden table nearby.

Rostnikov didn't answer. His eyes held those of the waiter.

"You are a policeman," Anton said. "Policemen are to be respected. We get many of them here. And it is my honor, as it was my father's before him, and my grandfather's, to be assigned to those of rank."

"I am not Chekhov," said Rostnikov.

"And," Anton said, standing, with no trace of irony, "I am not my grandfather."

Rostnikov nodded in agreement, and Anton departed, cradling in his cupped hand the table crumbs, which he bore like a delicate prize.

The Oreanda sanitarium was not far, but it was too far from the Lermontov Hotel for Sarah and Rostnikov to walk. There was a bus that made the rounds of the hotels and brought outpatients to the sanitarium twice each day. Normally, they took the late-afternoon bus. Today they managed to catch the morning bus, which was only ninety minutes late instead of the usual two and a half hours. They rode in bumpy silence, very much aware of other passengers: the silent ones, who looked out the window, pretending they had hope for their ailments; the resolute ones, with hope, who read books or let their eyes make contact with others.

"We should visit Alupka," Sarah said, touching her husband's hand.

"We should," he agreed, turning to her, intending to smile, but the smile was lost in a thought.

They said nothing more. When they reached the sanitarium, Rostnikov, as he always did, escorted her to the radiology section. He was about to take a seat next to her when she said, "Go. I'll meet you back here. I have a book."

She held up the book of poetry she had been carrying for weeks. The book was large, old, and tattered, with a red leatherlike cover. It had been a favorite book of Sarah's mother. Rostnikov knew that his wife had barely read it, that though she had been an insatiable reader before her surgery, it was almost impossible for her to read now, but the history, weight, and even the smell of the book gave her the comfort a child's doll or stuffed bear would give.

They were more than thirty years beyond the routine of his refusing to leave and her persuading him. He nodded, looked around at the other patients who were waiting, and left, trying to minimize his limp. For reasons that he did not wish to explore, Porfiry Petrovich did not want his limp to suggest that he was a patient.

He found Dr. Vostov at the swimming pool. He was sitting on a white-enameled chair, under a broad red-and-white umbrella on a stand, supervising therapy for an ancient quartet in the shallow water. Vostov, a round man of average height, with very curly black hair peppered with gray, was wearing sunglasses, which he had to lift up constantly because he was taking notes. Between notes, he watched a burly woman therapist in the water take the quartet through their routine.

"Dr. Vostov?" Rostnikov asked.

Vostov, absorbed in his work, looked up, surprised. His skin, Rostnikov could now see, was pale.

"I am Inspector Rostnikov, MVD."

Vostov seemed unsure about whether or not to rise. He started up and then changed his mind, lifting his sunglasses to take a look at the policeman.

"I'm supervising," Vostov said quite apologetically. "Would you like to sit while . . . ?"

"It is a bit difficult for me to get up and down," Rostnikov said. "Old injury. I would prefer for the moment to stand."

"You are a patient here?"

"No, my wife. Georgi Vasilievich was a . . . a colleague."

"Ah," said Vostov. "I see. Yes, I remember. He was some sort of government—" And then to the therapist in the water: "Work the legs, Ludmilla, the legs. Two more minutes."

His attention returned to Rostnikov, who stood patiently.

"Seawater in the pool," whispered Vostov. "Buoyant, curative. Seawater and very little sunshine. They come for the sun and sea air. They're half right. The sun will kill them. Show me a pale man or woman and I'll show you a potentially healthy person."

"Interesting theory," said Rostnikov. "Vasilievich's body. I would like to see it."

Vostov looked bewildered. He rose, tucking his notebook into a pocket of the white hospital jacket he wore open over a rumpled suit.

"I don't know if it is still here," said Vostov. "They

called and said they would like to pick it up this afternoon."

"They?" asked Rostnikov.

"Family," said Vostov. "At least I think so. I didn't talk to them."

"Let's look at the body," said Rostnikov.

"Two full minutes more, Ludmilla," Vostov called back as he moved away from the pool.

Ludmilla didn't bother to nod or answer.

Georgi Vasilievich's was not the only body in the cool white room.

"There are three others," Vostov whispered, moving past two waist-high carts on which bodies lay covered with sheets. "Sometimes there are none. Sometimes . . . you know. Old people, sick people."

"Yes," Rostnikov whispered as they approached the third cart.

Each morgue had its own rules, Rostnikov knew. Hospital rooms of death were equally divided between those in which you were expected to whisper and those in which you were not.

"Here," said Vostov, stopping in front of the third cart and pulling back the sheet.

Vasilievich was smiling. Rostnikov had seen many corpses, knew the rictus of death. This was not such a smile.

"Heart," said Vostov quietly. "Not fully unexpected."

Rostnikov pulled back the sheet, keeping Vasilievich's lower half covered. Vasilievich was a very hairy man. Vostov stood silently, sunglasses now in his breast pocket, while the policeman examined the hands of the corpse, turning them over.

"We will, of course, have him washed completely before his family—"

"Don't," said Rostnikov, moving to the foot of the table to examine the corpse's feet and legs.

"Don't . . . ?"

"Leave the body as it is," Rostnikov said softly. "Where are his clothes, the ones he was wearing?"

That Dr. Vostov did not know. He had to summon an aide, a very tall blond man with an enormous nose, who summoned an assistant, a woman with very thick glasses, who acted as if they had interrupted her in the middle of sex, which was highly unlikely, or food, which was a far greater possibility.

"He died peacefully," Vostov said with a little laugh as they waited, a laugh that was intended to convey that the policeman, who had asked that the body not be touched, was inappropriately thinking like a policeman, that Dr. Vostov had seen far more of death and knew it well and professionally.

"Where was he?" Rostnikov said, covering Georgi Vasilievich's face with the sheet. "Where was he found?"

"On a wooden deck chair facing the sea," Vostov said, pointing upward. "He must have gotten up early. Many of our patients have difficulty sleeping."

"Did anyone see him on the deck before his body was found?" asked Rostnikov. He was moving around the room now, slowly.

"No. You mean when he went out? No. He was found very early, and our—"

Vostov was cut short by the appearance of the woman with thick glasses, who dropped a duffel-bag-sized yellow plastic bag on an empty cart and walked out without a word.

"May I ask what you are looking for, Comrade Inspector?" Vostov asked, moving around to watch the policeman open the yellow bag and remove trousers, jacket, shirt, underwear, sox, and shoes, all of which he examined carefully as they spoke.

"You may."

"Then I'm asking," said Vostov, considering now the possibility that this barrel of a policeman was a bit dim-witted.

Rostnikov dropped the clothes back in the yellow bag.

"I want you to lock this bag someplace safe," said Rostnikov. "You will be held personally responsible. Then I want an autopsy."

Dr. Vostov could not control his sigh of exasperation. Less than a year ago one would not have dared to show exasperation with the police, but this was a new era that had touched even the Crimea.

"But, Inspector," he said as Rostnikov handed him the bag and moved to the door through which they had entered. "People die here almost every day. If we took the time to perform pathology—"

"He was murdered," said Rostnikov. "Please take me to his room."

"Murdered? No, no, no. He had a heart attack. I . . . ." Dr. Vostov moved in front of Rostnikov to face him. Rostnikov stopped and looked at the doctor patiently.

"There is dirt on the palms of both of Georgi Vasilievich's hands," Rostnikov explained as people passed them in the corridor. "That same dirt is on the knees of his trousers. It is not on his face. It is not on his shirt or jacket. When I saw him last night, shook his hand, it was clean, his pants were clean. At some point between the time he left my hotel and the time he was found dead, Vasilievich knelt on the ground with his palms in the dirt. Why would he do that?"

Dr. Vostov pondered the question and tried to come up with an answer, but he had none.

"That doesn't—" he began.

"There is also dirt on the back of his right hand and the knuckle of that hand—"

"He had arthritis," Dr. Vostov almost pleaded.

"The knuckle is broken on his middle finger," said Rostnikov.

"Broken?"

"Someone made Georgi Vasilievich kneel, put his hands out and his head down, and then they stepped on his hand. Take me to his room."

Dr. Vostov shook his head as if this were simply all wrong, as if, given a few moments, he could explain it all. He began walking to the stairway and then up.

"Why would anyone do that?" Vostov asked.

"To get him to tell them something," said Rostnikov, doing his best to keep up with the doctor, who now seemed to be in quite a hurry.

"Wait, wait. You mean some gang, kids, bums . . . Maybe they were just . . . maybe robbery, beating for fun," Vostov said. "It happens. Even here it happens. Kids from the city on vacation with their parents. Bored. Picking on the old people, the sick people," he went on, trying to keep the conversation quiet.

"They didn't take his wallet and money, and they

brought him back to the sanitarium. Not kids, not bums. They broke only one knuckle," Rostnikov said. "There isn't another bruise on his body. They tried pain and decided it wouldn't work. He wouldn't tell them. Then they killed him."

They were on the second floor now, moving down the corridor past curious patients, nurses, and cleaning staff.

"What did they want?" Vostov said. "No, no. With all respect, Inspector. I think . . . You know, sometimes professional people come for a vacation or treatment here, and miss their work. Architects see design, structural defects, in the hotels. Factory managers see inefficient management. That kind of thing. It's understandable. May I suggest—and I don't want to sound . . . I mean, the seawater and whirlpool baths would help your leg."

Vostov stopped in front of a door when they reached the end of the corridor. He shook his head and pushed the door open.

There was not much inside the small room, a metal clothes locker whose door stood slightly open, a chest with three drawers, all slightly open, a bed. On the wall there was the reproduction of a Cézanne harbor.

Rostnikov walked to the chest of drawers, opened them, and then closed each one. He moved to the closet, then the bed, and finally moved to the center of the room to simply stand with his hands folded in front of him and look around. He stood for more than a minute without speaking.

"Inspector . . ." Vostov began, looking around at the

room. This was now well beyond him. "I must get back to my patients."

"Someone searched this room and tried to make it look as if he or she did not," said Rostnikov, so softly that Dr. Vostov moved closer to catch a few words.

"What was that?" Vostov said.

"Nothing," answered Rostnikov, opening a drawer. The clothes were just slightly disheveled, the way a man living alone might throw them in a drawer, but Georgi Vasilievich was a humorless man who lived an ordered life, who would not tolerate a wrinkle in his bed covers or conversation.

Vostov was quite convinced now that the block of a man before him was one of the many who visited Yalta because they had suffered what the Americans called a "nervous breakdown." People being murdered, their rooms searched without a sign. It was nonsense.

"What were they looking for?" asked Vostov, as if he were humoring a small child.

"I don't know," said the policeman, "but I will find out. An autopsy now, Dr. Vostov, please."

"I don't think . . ." Vostov began, but Rostnikov turned, and their eyes met. "There is no reason, and the family might not—"

"Georgi Vasilievich had no family. His wife is dead. They had no children. Are you a married man, Doctor?" asked the inspector.

"Yes, but I . . ."

"Children?"

"One," said Vostov.

"Girl or boy?"

"Girl . . . woman," said Vostov. "She's thirty-five years old."

"Grandchildren?"

"Two," said Vostov.

"Pictures?" asked the inspector with a smile.

"Yes," said Vostov, reaching into his pocket and pulling out a wallet.

Vostov's eyes did not leave those of the inspector as he opened his wallet and turned it to show to Rostnikov.

"May I?" said Rostnikov, reaching for the wallet and adding, "My name is Porfiry Petrovich. And yours?"

"Ivan," said Vostov, letting Rostnikov take his wallet and examine the photograph.

"Boy looks strong, an athlete. Girl is very delicate."

"Vladim is twelve, plays soccer. Irina is ten."

"Ballet?" Rostnikov guessed, looking at the child's photo.

"Yes," said Vostov, accepting his wallet back.

"When I looked in Vasilievich's wallet, I saw two photographs: his GRU identification and a photo of him as a young man with his arm around the shoulder of a woman. My wife and I have one son, a grown son, too, not married," said Rostnikov, sighing deeply and looking once more around the room before ushering Vostov toward the door.

"Your son's name?"

"Iosef," said Rostnikov. "Just released from the army. Wants to work in the theater. Do you like working in Yalta, Comrade Vostov?"

They were walking back down the corridor now, in the same direction from which they had come.

Vostov shrugged.

"It's not Moscow," he said.

Rostnikov nodded in understanding.

"I sleep a great deal here even when I'm not tired," said Rostnikov as they came to the stairway and stepped out of the way to allow a pair of well-dressed, very young men to move past them.

"Some of it's the air," explained Vostov. "Some of it is letting down from the pressures."

"Georgi Vasilievich, I am sure, did many things of which he should not have been very proud. He leaves no one and nothing behind him, Ivan. He will be easy to forget. Too easy. Someone murdered him and did not try very hard to hide it. Someone murdered him and thought no one would care. And, Comrade Ivan Vostov, this offends me."

They reached the bottom of the stairs.

"I'll order the autopsy," said Vostov, following his own deep sigh.

The right corner of Rostnikov's mouth moved into a slightly lopsided smile, and he reached out to give the doctor an encouraging squeeze of the right arm, being careful not to cause even the slightest pain.

THREE

The grinning man with bad teeth standing in Yon Mandelstem's shower was a plainclothes policeman named Arkady Zelach, known to the other inspectors on the fourth floor of Petrovka as Zelach the Slouch. Arkady Zelach was a hulking, out-of-shape man who lived with his mother in the same small apartment in which he had been born forty-one years earlier. He had become a policeman because his father had been a policeman. He had never considering doing anything else, nor had his parents. Since he had neither brains nor intuition, Zelach relied totally on the judgment of his superiors and his mother, which made him quite valuable to both. He was loyal to his mother, whom he understood perfectly, and to Porfiry Petrovich Rostnikov, whom he understood not at all.

He grinned, not because he found the naked man in front of him, who was not really Yon Mandelstem, funny, but because it seemed the best face to wear when in doubt. People who didn't know him tended to think he was amused by something they had said or done. But that was only true of people who didn't know him.

"Why are you hiding in the shower?" asked Sasha Tkach, motioning Zelach out. Zelach moved to let Sasha reach in and turn on the shower.

"I didn't want anyone to know I was here," Zelach said while Sasha waited for the water to grow tepid enough to step under.

Tkach didn't bother to respond. He simply nodded and touched his face. He needed a shave.

"Go watch the door," Tkach said. "If someone breaks in, shoot them."

This Zelach understood.

The real Yon Mandelstem was a computer programmer with the Ministry of Labor in Leningrad. The apartment in Building Two of the Friedrich Engels Quartet had been obtained in the name of Mandelstem, who had been transferred to the Ministry of Labor in Moscow. However, the real Yon Mandelstem never got to Moscow, nor would he ever get there. He was in Saratov, using yet another name while he assisted for one week in the computer training of young men and women who would be operating the offices of McDonald's hamburger chain as it expanded throughout the Soviet Union. If anyone checked, they would find Sasha Tkach, with Mandelstem's identification, using Mandelstem's computer at Mandelstem's desk, though no one expected anyone to check. Following his week in Saratov, the real Mandelstem would leave the Soviet Union and immigrate to Israel. The papers had been prepared quickly and quietly, and he had been informed and told to pack within three hours for his trip to Saratov and then out of the country. Mandelstem, who looked very little like Sasha Tkach, had been quite willing to go, had even kept an emergency suitcase packed.

This, Sasha thought as the water went from cool to cold, was not the first time he had been away from Maya and the baby. In the past, there had always been the sense of temporary respite, primarily from Sasha's mother, Lydia, who had lived with them until just a month ago. Lydia had been the guilt and burden of his life.

Now Sasha and Maya and their daughter, Pulcharia, who was almost two, had their own apartment, and there was a new baby on the way. Times were uncertain, and there were those who still thought that a second child was foolish. Perhaps, he thought, they were right. In any case, he wanted to be home. He was thirty years old, no longer a boy, and he wanted to be home.

He scrubbed himself angrily. Rostnikov and Karpo were both on vacation, but he, he had to not only remain on duty but to stay away from his wife. The image of the woman, Tamara, in the lobby suddenly came to him, and in spite of the cool water, he found himself growing erect, which made him even angrier. He turned the metal handle all the way, but the water grew no colder nor the spray more powerful.

Think of the work, he told himself, scrubbing with the rough bar of soap he had brought with him from his and Maya's apartment. He forced himself to think about the other decoys in the field. He did not know how many there might be, but the Wolfhound had said there were others, others from different MVD branches, others with backup officers like Zelach.

There had been thirty reports of computer theft— breaking and entering apartments where people were known to have computers. Always apartments, never homes, always single men or women. And almost always Jews or people with names that might be considered Jewish. In seven cases, the break-ins had taken place while the computer owner was home. In all seven cases, the owner was beaten, beaten brutally. In not one case had a witness other than the victim been found who heard or saw anything in spite of the obvious noise. In none of the seven cases in which the victim had been present had any of them been willing to give a clear description of their assailants, for there was no way the police could protect them from retribution and all of them had been threatened with such retribution before they were beaten.

And so Sasha had been given a crash course in the computer, not enough to make him an expert but enough for him to do the work at the ministry, which he had done for almost two weeks, two weeks in which he had not seen his family, had only spoken to Maya three times by telephone, had only heard Pulcharia's voice once, saying, "*At'e'ts.* Father." Unbidden, he thought of Tamara again and grew even angrier. He shaved with the overused razor he had been using for a week and began to sing resolutely. Perhaps he would use his time to really master the computer. Perhaps he would ask to leave the MVD. There was probably no future in working for the Wolfhound. When Rostnikov had been demoted, Sasha had joined him because he wanted to continue to work with Rostnikov, but he also knew that in the end he had no choice. He was one of Rostnikov's men.

Sasha nicked his cheek. He sensed blood but ignored it, though he could not ignore the truth. He would not quit. It made little sense. Maya had said that it was because Sasha had never known his father that Rostnikov had become a father figure. Maybe, Sasha admitted, it was something like that.

He put the razor down on the little metal rack hanging from the shower head and rinsed off, being careful to place the precious bar of soap carefully back in the rack, where it would not be worn away by the shower water. A trickle of blood from his cheek joined the water going down the drain. He stopped singing abruptly and watched it dreamily. His hand reached up and turned off the water, but Sasha did not move. There was a mirror outside the shower, but he did not want to look. He touched the washcloth to his cut and tried to awaken from the trance.

When he pushed back the curtain, Zelach was standing there with a look of concern on his face.

"Are you all right?"

In fact, Zelach was the superior officer. In practice, they both knew that Sasha was in charge. Zelach had seen other policemen go into a zombie mode. It was usually the smart ones, the sensitive ones, like Sasha. When it happened, these officers were sent on vacations, from which some of them returned, while others went on to become clerks or bartenders.

"I'm fine," said Tkach, reaching for the towel on a hook outside the door.

"You're bleeding," said Zelach.

"I know," Sasha said, stepping out. "I'm fine. Go back in front of the door. I'm fine."

Zelach turned reluctantly and obeyed.

Sasha dried himself slowly and then wiped the moisture-covered mirror and looked at himself. On the surface it was an innocent, youthful face with a spot of blood on the left cheek. It was not a Jewish face, but many Jews he knew, including Rostnikov's wife, did not have faces that were particularly Jewish looking. He reached for the glasses and put them on. Even then he did not look Jewish, though he did look like a *sloo'-zhashchee*, an office worker, a bureaucrat. The thought depressed him. He dressed quickly, determined to go out and find a phone so that he could talk to Maya and hear Pulcharia's voice before her bedtime.

Yakov Krivonos looked down at Carla's body. Her red hair spread out, framing her face, and the blood dripping from her nostrils mingled with it. He would write a song about this moment, even though the dull streetlight robbed the scene of its true color.

It suddenly seemed very important that he remember Carla's last name. She had told him once. It was something like *No'veey got*, New Year. No, no, it wasn't. She was certainly dead, and since he had thrown her out the window, the least he could do was remember her last name. Looking down at her did nothing to help him. Someone behind him on the compact disc player shouted with joy. A breeze sucked in through the shattered window, trying to push Yakov gently back. He considered, seriously considered, leaping from the window ledge. He was almost certain he could fly, well, not quite fly, but keep himself suspended by will, moving slowly down. Yes, he could do it. He seemed to remember having done it before. He stepped onto the ledge.

Then he saw the face of death look up at him, and he hesitated. There, floating white below him, moving forward across the street, eyes fixed on him, the face floated in a sea of black. Perhaps if he jumped death would catch him.

He looked around for Jerold, almost called for him to come and see the face of death, but Jerold had dropped Carla and gone home. Yakov looked down again, and death was no longer there.

What had Carla done? It had only been seconds ago, and yet he couldn't remember what had caused him to push her through the window. It had something to do with . . . Yes, she had called him a name, but what name? What difference did it make?

Far away he heard the sound of a police siren. Amazing. Could they be coming this way already? Where had this sudden efficiency come from? Reluctantly, Yakov Krivonos stepped back from the window and looked around the room. It would be better to leave. He did not want to die before he saw Las Vegas, but what should he take with him?

He stepped over to the table and scooped most of the remaining capsules Jerold had left him into his palm and then plunged the handful into his pocket. He repeated this twice. The money on the table he folded over and stuffed in his rear pocket. His two-handled blue canvas bag with "Miami" emblazoned on it lay on the bed. He walked slowly to it, scooped it up, and moved to the CD player. Yakov began dropping the CDs into the bag. Music continued as he worked. It was, he thought, like a scene from *Miami Vice*. He had three videotapes of *Miami Vice*. Jerold had watched with him, telling Yakov what was happening. Yakov loved the dealers, the wild dealers, who took, killed, laughed. They were alive. The police on those shows were bores who triumphed not because they were better but because it was time to end each episode.

That was it. Yakov had what he needed. The sirens loomed closer. He moved to the window and looked down again. Three men and a woman stood around Carla's body. Another woman knelt at Carla's side.

"Leave her," Yakov shouted. "She looks beautiful."

They looked up at him, startled, transfixed.

Yakov shook his head at their stupidity. He rummaged through the bag of CDs, finding one by Sting. Carla had liked it. Yakov hated it. She could have it. He hurled it down, launching it with a flip of the wrist. The silver disc sailed past the windows below, skimmed the top of the car Carla had hit, and shot over the head of the kneeling woman. The people scattered, and Yakov wasn't sure whether to find another expendable disc, take another capsule, or just get out. He was reluctant to simply leave. Carla had given her life for this moment.

The other movie Jerold had shown him, the other one Jerold liked, the one with James Cagney. Jerold had said that Yakov looked like James Cagney. This did not please Yakov at first, but he had gradually grown used to the idea.

Yes, standing in this window, he was ready to explode. "Look, Mother. On top of the world," he shouted in English.

But Yakov was not going down with the building. He turned away from the window and headed for the door. The CD was still playing. How could that be? He had fought with Carla about it, and she had been dead for hours or minutes.

His hand was reaching for the knob when someone knocked once.

Yakov pulled his hand back as if the knob were white with heat. He knew who was at his door. Death was at his door. He should welcome Death. Better, he should kill Death. Then everyone would live forever. Rules would have to be made so there would be no more babies or the world would overflow.

Yakov looked at himself in the mirror next to the door, the mirror in which Carla spent so much time admiring herself. The gnome with orange hair arranged in five spiked points grinned at him. His orange shirt, which matched his hair, was buttoned at the collar, and his jeans were properly faded.

Death knocked again, and Yakov shouted, "Wait a moment. I'm thinking."

What would happen to someone you killed if Death died? This was profound. Jerold should hear it. If the sirens would stop, if the music would stop, if Death would be patient, Yakov would have the riddle of life solved. Before he was even eighteen, Yakov Krivonos would be famous, or he would be if he chose to be, if he chose to share his secret with the world.

"Fuck them," he said. "It's mine."

"Police," the voice of Death said. "Open the door."

Yakov reached into his canvas bag for a trick and came up with his Sturm .44mm Blackhawk revolver. Yakov had to put his canvas bag down so he could hold the nearly three-pound gun in both hands. He leveled the 7½-inch barrel at the door and waited for Death to knock again.

There was no knock, and Yakov sensed that he had little time. Death might not be so easy to stop. He put the revolver down and reached back inside the canvas bag for a second weapon, a compact rifle he held at his side, his left hand on the pistol grip, his right steadying the stock of the weapon.

He fired, holding the rifle steady, as Jerold had taught him. A hole appeared in the door, and the bullet sang across the hall and through the door of the next apartment. He fired again. Another hole. From outside in the hall a woman screamed, and a man shouted at her to shut up.

Yakov moved to the door and fired twice more. And then he opened it and stepped out. Death was not on the right but standing at the end of the corridor on the left, blocking the stairwell about twenty yards away, a small pistol aimed at Yakov, whose rifle hung at his side in his right hand.

"Drop the weapon," Death said, and Yakov sighed.

It wasn't really fair. Carla had been twenty-three. She had lived five years longer than Yakov would, for Yakov knew he would not drop the weapon, that he would lift it and aim and fire and that the man who was certainly Death would shoot him before he could do so.

The shot came before Yakov could get his weapon into both hands. It came howling over the nearby siren, the music, the crying woman in the apartment across the hall. Yakov paused. The bullet had gone through him or missed. There was no pain. Death turned and fired down the stairwell at his right. Yakov raised his rifle and aimed at Death, who stepped away from the stairwell, raised his right foot, and kicked at the door of an apartment. The doors, as Yakov knew, were made of thin pressed wood. He had kicked his in three times in the month he had been using the apartment. So it was no surprise that Death disappeared into the apartment as Yakov fired, blowing a fist-sized hole in the corridor wall.

"Yakov," Jerold called.

"Yes," Yakov called back, firing again.

Jerold stood at the top of the stairs, gun in hand. Jerold, so confident, a bearded aristocrat, a gangster, a real gangster, just as Yakov wanted to be. Jerold was teaching him many things, weapons, organization. Jerold was teaching him English so that Yakov could live in the United States, in Las Vegas, when it was over.

"Come on," Jerold called.

"My discs," Yakov called.

"No time," Jerold said calmly. "Come with me. We'll get more."

"You can't get Madonna," Yakov said, looking back at the apartment but walking toward Jerold. Tears were coming to his eyes. The loss of Madonna was too much to bear, was too unfair, given the miracles of this night.

"Yes, I can," said Jerold, who had his gun trained on the door of the apartment through which Death had plunged. "Let's go."

Something stirred inside the apartment. Jerold fired and nudged Yakov down the stairway.

"Hurry," Jerold commanded without the slightest sign of panic, although the police siren had stopped very close by.

Jerold covered their retreat to the next landing and urged Yakov down the hall to an apartment that was unfamiliar to the young man. Jerold tucked his pistol away, took out a key, opened the door, and ushered Yakov inside. The room was dark. Jerold closed and locked the door.

"Stand still," he said, and Yakov could hear Jerold's feet move across the wooden floor.

Yakov's stomach gave a first warning. He was coming down, coming down from whatever height he had reached with the help of the capsules. He did not want to come down. He wanted to remain in the dark and float, upside down, right side up, until there was no up or down. And then came a panic.

"Lights," he said. "Lights."

A light came on from a kitchen alcove on his left, and he could see Jerold, and behind Jerold he could see a woman seated at a small table. The woman's arms were taped together and then taped behind her head. Her legs were taped, too, as was her mouth. Her eyes were wide, tear-filled and frightened.

"Come," said Jerold, who turned to a window behind the woman.

Yakov moved past the woman, pausing to stare into her eyes. His nose almost touched hers, and he tried to smell her fear and see himself in those frightened eyes.

"Carla is dead," Yakov said in English, following Jerold to the window and slinging the rifle over his left shoulder. A wooden plank about two feet wide lay between this window and an open one in the next building, four feet away.

"I know," said Jerold softly, also in English. "I saw her. Go ahead."

"Shouldn't we kill her?" Yakov said, pausing to look at the woman, who whimpered.

"There's no reason," said Jerold. "The policeman saw us both."

"It was a policeman," said Yakov with a laugh, gripping the shoulder strap of the rifle. "I thought it was Death."

"Crawl," said Jerold.

And Yakov went through the window, and over his shoulder and the barrel of the rifle, against which he rubbed his cheek, he whispered, "You can get Madonna?"

"Yes," said Jerold. "You'll have much more than Madonna after Thursday. Just be ready."

"Walther and I will be ready," Yakov said. "We will be ready."

FOUR

The food at the Lermontov Hotel was all right for quantity. Anton saw to that when Sarah and Porfiry Petrovich entered the dining room. He flitted from the Rostnikovs to the American couple who had checked in three days before to the Sabolshevs from Minsk to the twig of a man who spoke with an accent that Rostnikov recognized as Romanian.

"Anton works hard for his tips, Porfiry Petrovich," Sarah said. "We should remember that when we go."

She was holding her plate in front of her. On the plate was a mound of something dark, a treacherous hill of kasha, mystery vegetables, and small, dark, jagged pieces that may have been meat. The entire creation was topped with a tiny cap of barely cooked dough. At the base of this mountain was a thin white sauce in which floated two very thin slices of tomato. Rostnikov's plate was identical, as were the plates of all forty-six people in the room.

"This way," Rostnikov said, nodding toward a table near the window where the new American couple sat, forks in hand, glasses of *pee'va*, tepid beer, near their plates of food.

The man looked up as Sarah and Rostnikov approached.

"Have a seat," the man, who had two chins and very white hair, said.

Rostnikov and Sarah put down their plates and sat.

"You speak English?" the man asked.

"Yes," said Rostnikov.

"What the hell is this stuff?" he said, pointing at the mound in front of him with his fork.

"Lester," his wife, a thin woman with dyed blond hair, whispered.

"I'm curious, is all," Lester said.

"I think it is *chebureki*, an Armenian meat pie fried in fat," said Rostnikov.

"Appetizing," said the man, with a frown.

"Lester," said the wife, trying not to move her lips, as if her act of inept ventriloquism would hide her words from the Rostnikovs. "You don't need to offend—"

"Am I offending you?" Lester said, looking at Sarah and Porfiry Petrovich.

"We did not cook the food," Rostnikov answered.

"See," said Lester. "They don't like it, either."

The subdued chatter in the room was broken by the sound of a concertina.

"Oh, hell, no," groaned Lester. "She's back."

"Lester," his wife warned, looking apologetically at Sarah, who was much more discomfited by the American woman's embarrassment than by Lester's complaints.

"Is that native Crimean music?" Lester asked, leaning over toward Rostnikov to be sure he was heard over the noise of the concertina playing a particularly bad version of a folk song Rostnikov recognized but could not name.

"I don't know," said Rostnikov.

Sarah was picking at her food. Rostnikov had almost downed the entire mound.

"Look at her," Lester said in disgust, pointing his chins at the concertina lady.

Rostnikov dabbed at his mouth with his napkin and turned to look at the slightly overweight woman in a generic native costume. Her face was round, overly made up, her mouth fixed in a huge smile, in contrast with her eyes, which looked pained.

"She's not bad," said Lester's wife, looking for support from Sarah and Rostnikov.

"She is trying," said Rostnikov.

"It's damn painful," said Lester. "This is the nightly entertainment they promised us? Every night that poor creature comes in playing the same songs and ending with the national anthem of the day. If she tries 'The Star-Spangled Banner' tonight, I'm walking the hell out. The woman is depressing. Every night I've been here I've gone to bed depressed."

"Tomorrow we go to the Nikitsky Botanical Garden," said the wife, trying to change the subject.

Sarah nodded politely, though she was having great difficulty picking up enough of the English to truly understand.

"Our son lives in St. Louis, two blocks from one of the biggest botanical gardens in the United States," said the man. "We go to St. Louis every year, and we haven't had the slightest interest in seeing the botanical gardens once in eleven years. Now I go five thousand miles to see the same trees and flowers I could have seen at home."

The concertina lady stopped. While she engaged in her nightly ritual of trying to get some of the disgruntled diners to dance, Lester leaned over the table and held out his hand.

"Lester McQuinton," he said.

"Porfiry Petrovich Rostnikov," Rostnikov said, taking the huge hand.

Rostnikov was not surprised by the strength of the man's grip. In spite of the fat, Lester McQuinton's arms were solid, his chest large. It was clear, however, that Lester McQuinton was surprised by the grip of the compact man across from him.

"My wife's Andrea. We call her Andy," said Lester, nodding at his wife but keeping his eyes on Rostnikov, for whom he had developed a sudden respect.

"My wife is Sarah," said Rostnikov. "She speaks very little English."

"Sorry about that, but hell, I don't speak any Russian. Never had any call to. This is the only time we've been out of the States."

"We have never left the Soviet Union," said Rostnikov.

"I'm a police officer," said Lester McQuinton. "New York Police Department."

"I, too, am a police officer," said Rostnikov. "Moscow."

"I could tell. You've got the look. I see it in the mirror every morning. You people having a convention here or something?" asked Lester as the concertina started again.

"I'm sorry?" said Rostnikov.

"Ran into one of you guys on the hotel bus yesterday in the morning," said Lester. "Lonely-looking guy. Introduced myself and Andy. He was surprised I knew he was a cop, but, like I said, I can spot one whether he's named Ivan or Al. You know what I mean?"

"We were coming back from the Marble Palace, where Stalin, Roosevelt, and Churchill met after the war," Andy added, addressing Sarah directly. "Beautiful collection of modern art."

"I'm not keen on modern art," McQuinton said, considering another try at his food and deciding against it.

"I, too, am not filled with affection for modern art," said Rostnikov, "but my wife admires it."

"Maybe we could do something together tomorrow, go into town? I understand there's an art museum," Andy McQuinton said, looking at Sarah.

Rostnikov started to translate for Sarah, but she stopped him and said she understood. Sarah smiled at Andy, who smiled back.

"My wife says she would be happy to do something with you. Do you remember his name, the policeman on the bus?" Rostnikov asked. "Was it Vasilievich, Georgi Vasilievich?"

He was not sure how much of the conversation Sarah understood, but she looked up from her food when she heard her husband say, "Vasilievich, Georgi Vasilievich?"

"Don't remember the name," said Lester. "You, Andy?"

"No," she said, working on her tomatoes.

"I don't think it was *Vaslich* or anything like that," said Lester. "I'm not coming here for dinner tomorrow night. There must be someplace better to eat. I don't care if it is part of the damn tour package."

"A man of almost seventy," Rostnikov tried. "Thin, knuckles with arthritis, and—"

Lester was shaking his head no. Rostnikov stopped.

"No offense, but I think you people may have nothing better to do than watch each other. Over by the pillar behind you," said Lester. "The bald guy sitting alone. The cop from the bus."

Rostnikov decided at that moment that Lester McQuinton was probably a very good policeman. The American's eyes had not betrayed his knowledge of the bald man, had not looked in his direction. Porfiry Petrovich was well aware that behind him in a far corner, sitting alone, was a pear of a man with very little hair remaining on his head. The man had a large nose, a vodka nose. His eyes, Rostnikov had observed, were quite large. And even though the man was doing a very good job of not looking directly at him, Rostnikov had observed his reflection fleetingly, though carefully, in both the dusty glass that covered a fading seascape on the lobby wall and in the large, uneven mirror just inside the door of the dining room as he had entered with Sarah.

The man had been both observing and following Rostnikov for the past two days. It was not the first time he had been followed in his career, nor was it a surprise. Rostnikov assumed that it was the KGB again. He had run afoul of them more often than it was safe to do so, and from time to time, to remind him that his past indiscretions were not forgotten, a KGB agent would follow him for a few days and take no particular pains to remain unseen.

Rostnikov had assumed this was one of those times, but since the death of Vasilievich and his preliminary investigation, he was no longer sure.

"You knew he was there, didn't you?" asked Lester McQuinton with a grin. "You didn't bat an eye, turn your head, or twitch."

"I was aware of his presence, yes," said Rostnikov, reaching for his glass of wine and taking a drink that finished the glass. "Please excuse me. I will be back shortly."

He touched Sarah gently on the back as he rose.

As Rostnikov headed in the general direction of the rest rooms and the woman with the accordion made a fool out of a fat American she had coaxed out to dance, McQuinton nibbled at his food, chewed on his bread, and pretended to listen to Andy and the Russian cop's wife trying to carry on a conversation. He watched the Russian cop make his way through the crowd and the bald guy pretend not to watch him.

The Russian cop was interesting. He was the only truly interesting thing he had encountered since he left New York. The doctors hadn't fooled him, and they hadn't fooled Andy. Lester and Andy didn't believe their words of hope because the doctors themselves didn't and weren't street smart enough to fool a thirty-year detective who spent too much of his time dealing with lies. Andy had half a year, maybe a little more or less. And she had wanted this trip, less because she wanted to travel than that she wanted the distraction and because she couldn't bear staying in New York and watching him observe her. She had accepted it eagerly when he suggested it.

He had complained since the beginning, for he wanted this to be a perfect trip for her. He complained because he was angry. He complained because it was normal to do so and he didn't want Andy to feel that he was doing anything but being normal. None of it had worked. Until now.

He could tell from the eyes of the Russian cop's wife that she sensed something of what Andy and he were going through. Well, maybe not everything, but enough. For the moment, the burden of being responsible for his wife's happiness had eased, and the game the Russian cop with the bad leg was playing focused his attention on something besides Andy.

A cackling laugh came from a woman to McQuinton's right. The laughter turned to choking, and someone, a man, he thought, began to scold the choking woman in Russian. The woman managed to control herself and the accordion squealed into a tune that may have been "Fascination."

McQuinton admired the way Rostnikov weaved through the crowd and made the turn around the corner toward the rest rooms. The bald guy didn't follow, didn't move. Why should he? The cop had left his wife at the table. The cop with the bad leg was obviously going to the toilet. The man watching was good. He didn't let up. He ate, drank, kept his head down, and let his eyes take in the entire room. But the cop with the bad leg was better. He was back in seconds, much too fast to have reached the toilet. He headed directly for the bald man and even with the bum leg got to him before he could get all the way up. The cop put his right hand on the bald guy's shoulder like an old friend in friendly conversation, but McQuinton knew the bald guy was trying to rise and was being stopped by the pressure. Lester's respect for the cop with the bad leg went up another notch. He was keeping the man down with one hand and almost no effort.

"We can do that, can't we, Lester?" Andy said.

"Sure," said Lester, though he had paid no serious attention to the conversation of the two women.

The Russian cop with the bad leg was sitting next to the bald man now. They were talking like two strangers who strike up a conversation while hanging on to bus straps on the way home from work and find they have something in common. Lester smiled.

Behind the two Russians Lester McQuinton was watching, two men appeared in the open doorway that led to the lobby. They were an odd couple—a giant and a nervous little man who looked at Lester and then at Rostnikov. The smile left Lester McQuinton's face.

One of the privileges of being a policeman in Moscow was having a phone in your apartment. One of the disadvantages of being a policeman in Moscow was that you were seldom at home to use it.

Maya answered after the first ring, actually before the first ring had even ended. Sasha had been standing at the lonely booth at the corner across from the park, trying every three minutes to call his number. He had been trying for half an hour when he finally got through.

"It's me," Sasha Tkach said, trying to hide his irritation.

"The baby just fell asleep," Maya whispered. "A few minutes ago."

"I wanted to say good night to her," he said. "Your phone has been busy."

"Your mother, Lydia," said Maya, and that was all that needed to be said. "Are you all right?"

"Yes," he said.

"Did you eat?"

"Yes," he said.

He wanted to tell her that he was filled with frustration. They had spent only four nights in the apartment together. He wanted to make love to her without worrying about his mother listening in the next room. He wanted to hear her purr like a cat when he rubbed her back. He wanted to cover her wide mouth and full lips in his and lose himself in her. He wanted her to keep talking, for he loved her voice, her Georgian accent, and he dreaded the walk back to Zelach and the apartment in Engels Four. He wanted to say these things, but instead he heard her say, "Sasha?"

"Yes."

"I have to work early tomorrow."

Maya worked in the day-care center for mothers in the Ts UM department store. She brought Pulcharia with her when she worked and put in as many hours as she could. A new baby was coming. Seven months away. Sasha had hoped for intimate months together before Maya was too large and uncomfortable.

"I'm sorry I'm keeping you," he said with sarcasm. "I'll hang up and let you get some sleep."

"I wasn't trying to say I wanted to go to sleep," she said. "I was . . . You weren't talking. I was just telling you."

The movement was slight, a change in the light dancing off the leaves of the bushes fringing the cement path. It could have been many things, but it wasn't. It was a person. Sasha sensed it before he knew with certainty. But he had almost missed it. He had almost lost himself in the conversation with Maya, a conversation he should not be having. He had been ordered specifically to make no contact with his friends or family for the duration of the operation.

"I'm sorry," he said, turning his back on the movement in the bushes and holding up his wristwatch as if he were weary of the conversation and checking the time. Sasha pretended to adjust the watch and flipped the supple band so the back of the watch was facing him, the shiny back of the watch in which he could see the bush as he put his hand up to lean on the side of the phone booth.

"Get some sleep, Sasha," Maya said.

"I will," he said. "You, too. And kiss Pulcharia in her sleep."

The man moved carefully from behind the bush. He was large, appeared to be young, and was wearing dark slacks and a dark sweater. He ducked behind a second bush, somewhat closer to Sasha. A second man, with

long blond hair and a blond beard, followed the first
man. Sasha lowered his arm.

"I'm not tired, Sasha," Maya said. "We can talk if
you like."

"Tomorrow, Maya," he said. "I have to go."

"Good night," she said. "I love you."

"And I love you," Sasha said.

Maya hung up the phone, but Sasha continued to
talk, turning as the men worked their way closer to
him. Sasha had no gun. He was supposed to carry one,
but less than three years earlier he had shot a boy during a robbery of a government liquor store. The image
of the moment in which Sasha's eyes had met those of
the boy, who was only sixteen, haunted Tkach. But
what was worse, Sasha found that he could not remember the boy's face. For almost a year he had searched
the faces of young men he encountered on the street,
hoping that a face would bring back a vivid memory,
but it did not happen. Tkach carried no gun, and he
knew the two men were making their way toward him.

"No," Tkach said aloud now so that they could hear
him. "I've got to be at work. Why? Because I'm the
only one who can handle the program. You think any
fool can deal with a computer program like that?"

Sasha rummaged through his mind to find some work
phrase that would be particularly Jewish, a phrase that
would be right for Yon Mandelstem, but he could come
up with none. He settled for an inflection, a movement
of the shoulders and arms that he had observed in his
former neighbor, Eli Houseman.

"Then you don't, Eli," Sasha said. "I'm sorry for
you."

A group of women suddenly burst through the bushes not ten yards from where the two men watching Sasha Tkach were hidden. The women were laughing; two of them were holding hands. Sasha recognized the woman Tamara, whom he had met in the hall of Engels Four a few hours earlier.

"Good-bye, Eli," he said vehemently, and hung up the phone.

He turned as if irritated by his call and let his eyes meet those of the woman who was looking at him. Sasha smiled and stepped onto the path so that the quartet of women would meet him.

Tamara held out her arms to stop her companions, one of whom was very young, perhaps eighteen, and trying to look much older, which only succeeded in making her look even younger than she was.

"Ah," Tamara cried, "there he is, the one I told you about. *Mon petit Juif.*"

The woman's French accent was weak, much weaker than that of Sasha, who pretended that he did not know she had called him her little Jew.

The women giggled, and Tamara stepped forward. "Out for a walk?" she asked.

Sasha looked directly at her but saw the movement of the men in the bushes as they stepped back into deeper darkness.

"Yes," he said. "I couldn't sleep."

"Maybe you'd like that drink?" she asked.

Her friends giggled. She turned to them with a warning look.

"I'd like it," Sasha said.

Tamara took his arm and moved out along the path.

"Tell us about it tomorrow, Tamma," one of the women shouted.

"I hear they tickle," another woman added.

Sasha pretended not to hear as Tamara waved her friends away and led him toward the buildings. Sasha turned his head and smiled, looking back at the trio of women behind but seeing along the path, in the light of a lamp, the two men, perhaps fifty yards away. They may have been looking at the three women. At least a passerby would assume so, but Sasha knew that their eyes were on him.

He smiled and let Tamara take him. She smelled of cheap makeup, alcohol, and woman, and she held him as if he were a prize she had captured in the park, her little Jew, the trophy. Guilt, relief, and excitement ran through him. As the Jew he pretended to be, he despised this woman. As the man he pretended to be, he needed her protection. And as Sasha Tkach, he felt the softness of her left breast against his arm through her dress.

"They were going to kill me," said Elena Kusnitsov.

She was sitting in her kitchen chair, the same chair the man named Jerold had tied her to and from which the police had released her. When the tape had been removed, Elena Kusnitsov had tried to rise, but her left knee began to dance, and she had to sit down. It had continued to bounce up and down unbidden, as if hearing a tune the rest of Elena could not appreciate. She had tried to use her hands to stop the dance and had succeeded, at least for the moment.

It was bad enough to be frightened, to have to face killers, to have to sit here with this ghost of a policeman hovering over her, but to suffer the humiliation of this mad, frightened foot of hers was enough to bring tears to her eyes. Elena did not want to cry, certainly not in front of this policeman, who stood there patiently waiting for his witness's leg to cease its spasms.

Elena, who was sixty-three, quite mistakenly prided herself on her ability to appear forty. She dyed her hair, watched her weight, wore clothes she believed were fashionable, and made up her face carefully each morning, after lunch, and immediately after coming home from her job at the Beriozka, the Birch Tree, dollar shop in the Metropole Hotel. She was a woman of culture who could sell American cigarettes or Russian vodka in three languages. She talked to important people from foreign countries every day. Wearing the very dress she was now wearing, she had spoken to Armand Hammer, the wealthiest American in the world. This should not happen to her. She looked at her knee and felt her eyes fill with tears.

"I'm not doing this on purpose," she explained.

"I know that," said Emil Karpo. "We can wait."

Elena did not want to wait. She wanted this frightening creature out of her small apartment.

"When you go, I will close that window, the window through which the two had climbed. I will close it and nail it shut. Never mind Popkinov. I don't care if he is the district maintenance officer. I don't care if he is a party member. I don't care if you are a party member," she said, trying to sound defiant.

"I am a party member," said Karpo.

"I don't care. Boris Yeltsin, our president, quit the party," Elena Kusnitsov said.

The knee. The damnable knee. When would it stop? When would he leave? The noise of ambulances, police cars, curious people outside looking at the body the policeman told her was there, those noises had not stopped. They came through the open window and contributed to both Elena's fear and defiance.

Karpo leaned over and reached down toward Elena with his left hand.

Elena released a tiny whimper and cringed, almost falling backward in her chair.

"No," she said.

There was no point in Emil Karpo explaining that he simply wanted to reassure the woman, calm her down so that he could get information from her. Rostnikov would have had her quiet long ago, would have had her eager to cooperate, but Rostnikov was not here, and Karpo had a criminal to pursue.

Elena's knee had stopped dancing. She smiled up at Karpo, her makeup a smear, her hair wild, and then the tears came.

Karpo waited patiently while she sobbed.

"Ask," she said through her tears.

"I can wait," said Karpo.

"I want to answer, and I want you to leave," Elena said through her sobs. "My father was construction foreman on the Moskva Swimming Pool. This should not happen to me."

"Did the two men speak?" Karpo asked, taking out his notebook.

"Yes," she said, brushing back her hair with her right hand. "I look terrible."

"What did they say?"

"They didn't know I understood them," said Elena. "I speak three languages in addition to Russian."

She looked up at Karpo to see if he would challenge her.

"What language did they speak?"

"English," she said. "The young one with the orange hair spoke very bad English. The other one, the older one with a beard, he was American."

"What did they say?"

"Nonsense, they said. They are crazy people. Crazy people speak nonsense. The one with orange hair put his face right in front of mine. He wanted to kill me. He told the other one to get him a Madonna."

"What else?" asked Karpo.

"Jerold," she said. "The American one with the beard was Jerold."

Karpo didn't bother to say, "What else?" He simply stood, pen poised, and waited while Elena wiped her eyes with the back of her left hand and looked around.

"Thursday," she said. "The American one, Jerold, told the other one to take it easy, that he had to be ready for Thursday. And the one with the orange spikes said he would be ready. That Walther would be ready."

"Walther?" asked Karpo.

"Yes. You know who Walther is?" she asked.

"Walther is a gun," Emil Karpo said.

The door to Elena Kusnitsov's apartment suddenly

burst open. She screamed, and her knee began to dance again. A young man in a brown policeman's uniform, carrying a black weapon that he held in two hands, entered.

"What are you doing?" she screamed. "This is my apartment. It may not be much, but it is mine. Just because two lunatics broke in doesn't give everyone the right to break in."

The young policeman looked at Karpo, who gave him no help, and then at the woman.

"I'm sorry," he said.

"I've been violated," she screamed.

The young policeman took a step backward.

"What is it?" Karpo asked the young man.

"You are to report to Colonel Snitkonoy at Petrovka immediately, Comrade Inspector," the policeman said.

"Violated," Elena repeated.

The policeman backed out of the room quickly and disappeared. Karpo tore a sheet from his notebook and handed it to Elena Kusnitsov, who took it carefully, as if it were extended bait and he might suddenly reach out and grab her.

"It's the name of a lock for your door and window," he said, putting his notebook away. "I've written where you can buy them and the name of a woman who will install them for you. No one will be able to pick or break the locks."

Karpo didn't add that a determined assailant could break down the door or smash the window. The lock could not keep someone out, but the need to make noise might be sufficient to make a burglar consider another door.

"Thank you," Elena said, carefully placing the sheet of paper in her lap as if it were a fragile wineglass.

"A policeman will remain in the building all night," he said. "The two men will not be coming back."

"But others might," she added quickly.

"Statistics do not support that likelihood," he answered, moving toward the door.

"But they exist," she said triumphantly.

"They exist," he admitted, and went into the hall.

FIVE

"We can go to your apartment if you prefer," Tamara whispered, holding Sasha's arm tightly as they went up the stairs, breathing in his ear. "I can get my bottle and bring it."

"No," said Sasha, wondering what Zelach and Tamara might think and say if they suddenly faced each other in the small apartment.

He had a very simple plan. He would go with Tamara to her apartment, remember something he had to work on, make his excuses, and depart. Maybe he would have one drink. How could it hurt? The men who he thought were watching him were probably just muggers, not the computer thieves. Moscow was filled with muggers who roamed confident that the police were too busy with more important crimes occasioned by Gorbachev's reforms to deal with a little mayhem and the loss of a few rubles here and there.

Sasha deserved a drink, a moment to relax. He seldom drank and didn't intend to now, but the idea of one drink, a few moments watching Tamara, having her hold his arm, was appealing. It could cause no harm. Zelach was sitting behind the door ready if someone came while Sasha was out.

I could even argue that I had left intentionally, he told himself. Left to lure the thieves into breaking in so Zelach could catch them.

"This is the door," Tamara said with a big grin, showing her teeth. The center tooth had just a spot of lipstick on it.

"I've got to get back to my apartment," Sasha said, trying to remove the woman's hand from his arm. She held fast.

"One drink," she said, searching for her key in the little purse she carried with her free hand. "A moment. I'm afraid to go in by myself. Just go in with me. I'll turn on the lights, and and then you can go if you want."

"I can stand in the hall," said Sasha, adjusting his glasses.

"You're cute," she said. "My shy little Jew."

Tamara opened the door with one hand, the other still holding tightly to Sasha, tugging at him as she entered. He told himself that he had no choice but to follow.

"The light's here," Tamara said, kicking the door shut behind them.

For an instant she released Sasha's arm and left him standing in the darkness, penetrated only by a faint light through the window from the street below. Then the light came on. The room was bright, a room of yellows and reds, the furniture modern and colorful, with flowers, and the rug a large yellow rectangle with a red rose the size of Maya's favorite mixing bowl in the center.

"I must go now," Sasha said.

Tamara smiled at him from where she stood across the room near a floor lamp.

"If you have to work, you have to work," she said with a shrug, kicking off her shoes and moving toward him with her right hand held out. As she neared, he held out his hand to take hers, to shake it quickly, to make a hurried departure and get back to Zelach, who was probably asleep and snoring in the chair behind the door.

Tamara ignored his extended hand, moved in, and put her arms around his neck and her open mouth on his. Sasha took her arms to remove her, but she had her hands locked behind his neck. He opened his mouth to tell her he really had to leave, but her tongue entered, licking his lower teeth before he could speak.

She tasted of warmth and alcohol, a sweet, different taste from Maya.

"Maybe another night," he said as she released her grip and stood back to look at him with a knowing smile. "Tomorrow."

Her right hand moved forward suddenly between his legs. He backed away but had only a half step to the door. Her hand pressed forward.

"Tonight," she said, moving in, releasing his belt.

Sasha wanted to speak, opened his mouth again, but Tamara said, "Shhh," and unbuttoned his pants.

This must stop. Now. He must halt her firmly, his mind ordered, but his mesmerized body would not obey. Her fingernails rubbed against the flesh at his

waist, not quite gently, promising, threatening. He said
no more as she dropped his pants to the floor and put
her thumbs inside his underwear. It was too late. There
was no point in issuing orders to his body. His underwear came down to his knees, and Tamara stepped back
to look at him.

Her hands went to her hips, and she asked, "Are you
sure you're a Jew?"

Colonel Snitkonoy had exhausted his complete array of
poses, and none of them had worked on Emil Karpo,
who sat impassively alone at the conference table and
looked up at him. Had it been daylight, the colonel
could have set this meeting with Karpo for the precise
moment the sun hit the window. Then, the Gray Wolfhound knew, he would be outlined in light, a tall figure
with bright filaments of red and yellow stabbing into
the room. His voice, carefully nurtured, would resonate
in baritones off the walls. It would have been a concert
of light and sound to which few failed to respond.

But this was very early in the morning, before five,
before the sun. Before Karpo had arrived, the
Wolfhound had turned on the two floor lamps in the
corners of the office and the one lamp that reflected
upward from the well-polished top of his oak desk to
create deep shadows around the eyes and below the
lips. Aware of every crease and button on his perfectly
pressed uniform, the colonel had moved from one light
to the other since Karpo had entered the room. Erect,
hands clasped behind his back, the Wolfhound found
the right nuance of light for the right phrase. Nothing.

But it was difficult to discourage Colonel Snitkonoy. Some said it was impossible. He had too much confidence. Others had suggested that he did not have the intellect to merit such confidence.

It was the great confidence and lack of intellect of Colonel Snitkonoy that had sustained him in the MVD for over thirty years while others fell or were trampled. It was the sense of the theatrical and the imposing figure he presented that had moved him to his present position as director of special projects. He was until recently, it was generally agreed, no threat to anyone.

The irony of Colonel Snitkonoy's current rise in party circles was that his department, a repository of largely ceremonial duties no other branch wanted, had met with singular success. During what appeared to be a routine investigation of a minor problem at a shoe factory, Rostnikov had uncovered a high-ranking KGB officer engaged in extortion. And then Rostnikov and Tkach, while on a routine check of parade security, had foiled a terrorist attempt to destroy Lenin's tomb. Colonel Snitkonoy's star had risen, and now there were some who said that he had been a brilliant survivor who waited for years to build a superior staff and to seize the moment when it was safe to become dangerous.

Whatever the truth, greater autonomy and responsibility had come to the colonel's staff and with it possible enemies. Colonel Snitkonoy was learning what it was like to be vulnerable. He was also reaping the rewards of success, and in just two days he would, as the guest of Gorbachev himself, attend a ceremony in Soviet Square followed by a dinner to honor those who were contributing selflessly to the success of *perestroika* and peaceful transition.

"Inspector Karpo, Comrade Karpo," he said, deciding to try compassion, "a young woman is dead. I grant that. I lament that. The loss of any Soviet citizen, especially a youthful citizen who holds promise for the future, is of great concern to Colonel Ivan Snitkonoy."

"There is nothing to lament, Colonel," said Karpo, looking up. "The young woman was Carla Wasboniak, a user and seller of drugs, a probable accessory to several murders, an enemy of the state."

"Yet you feel compelled to find the young man who killed her," said the Wolfhound tolerantly, a wiser figure with perfectly groomed silver hair who' was sure, now, that the pale figure seated before him would see the weakness in his position.

"His name is Yakov Krivonos," said Karpo. "We have sufficient evidence to believe he has murdered three people, possibly more. He is quite mad, quite dangerous. Inspector Rostnikov and I believe that he was involved in the murder of the visiting German businessman last month."

"Bittermunder?" said the Wolfhound, perplexed but not showing it in the least as he nodded as if he knew where this conversation was going. "Senseless, very brutal."

"Yes," said Karpo.

"Why?"

"Why was he murdered, or why does Inspector Rostnikov believe Krivonos is involved?" asked Karpo without a trace of sarcasm.

The colonel, like most people, had avoided conversation with Emil Karpo as much as possible. He had always been confident that when the time came he could deal with this creature of the night if necessary. He had always told himself, however, that it was easier to allow Rostnikov to deal with the man. After all, Karpo had worked for years with Rostnikov when they were in the Procurator General's Office, and Rostnikov did not seem to mind the man, even seemed to have some genuine affection for him, which was a mystery to the Gray Wolfhound.

"Answer both if you can," the colonel said with a tiny smile that suggested superior amusement and masked a confusion.

"The weapon," said Karpo. "The bullets taken from the German's body were 76.2-millimeter Winchester Magnum cartridges fired from a high-powered West German sniper rifle, a Walther WA2000. Such a rifle was stolen from the collection of the deputy director of Social Mobilization for the Russias a week earlier. An informant told Inspector Rostnikov that a young man named Yakov Krivonos was making the rounds of underground bars where American music is played, bragging that he had such a weapon, that he had killed a German with it. We attempted to find Yakov Krivonos but were unable to do so. He was in hiding, but I persuaded a bartender in the Billy Joel—"

"Billy Joel?" the colonel repeated, shaking his head.

"A rock-music establishment," Karpo explained. "Named for the American singer who came here last year."

"Yes," said the colonel. "Go on."

"I persuaded a bartender to tell me that Yakov Krivonos was known to have a companion named Carla. I waited until she showed up at the bar last night and then followed her to the apartment from which she was thrown."

"Or fell," Colonel Snitkonoy amended.

"She landed on the rear streetside fender of an automobile approximately fifteen feet from the building," Karpo said. "I watched her descent and—"

"I have been informed," said the colonel, looking toward the window in the vain hope that the sun was finally rising. A childhood memory came back, and he thought that perhaps the first rays of the sun would destroy this vampire. The colonel admitted to himself that he was quite tired.

"The rifle Krivonos fired at me this night was a Walther 2000, the same make as that which was stolen," Karpo went on. "It is likely that the bullets I retrieved and have given to the laboratory will verify that it is the same weapon that killed Bittermunder."

"I see," said the Gray Wolfhound, resuming his pacing, since intimacy had no effect.

"We do not know," Karpo went on.

"Know? Know what?"

"The answer to your second question. Why Yakov Krivonos murdered Bittermunder."

"Ahh," said the colonel. "But really, it doesn't matter. This is murder, a foreign visitor. It is a case for the Murder Squad and not Special Projects."

"On Thursday, Yakov Krivonos will kill again," said Karpo without emotion. "A witness heard him say this to his companion, a man with a beard whom he called

Jerold. I saw this Jerold for an instant when he shot at me."

It was more than the colonel cared to keep track of.

"I will try to find Yakov Krivonos before Thursday and stop him from committing this murder," said Karpo.

"You are, as you may remember, on vacation as of tomorrow," the Wolfhound said softly, with just the slightest studied tone of warning.

"I am the only police officer who can identify Yakov Krivonos," Karpo said.

"A young man with orange spiked hair and wild clothing is not difficult to describe to others," the colonel tried.

"He will change his appearance," said Karpo.

"He will change his appearance," the colonel repeated, as if humoring a dense child. "How do you know this?"

"I saw the face of the man with the beard," he said. "The man called Jerold will tell him to do it, and he will do it."

"It is late, Comrade Karpo," the colonel said, taking out the 1920 pocket railroad watch that had been given to him in 1972 by the workers of the Kirov Locomotive Assembly Plant after a particularly inspiring speech on the need for maintaining domestic security. "With the increase in crime since . . . certain political events, too many hours have been put in by all branches. We must all be alert, ready, refreshed for the arduous task of maintaining the peace and controlling crime. You will take a vacation beginning tomorrow. That is a directive from the General Staff. When you and Porfiry Petrovich return, Tkach and Zelach will also be directed to take vacations. You will visit your relatives in Kiev. You will return in three weeks and not before then. You will return with renewed vitality. You understand my words?"

"Yes, Comrade Colonel," Karpo said, noting that the offer to use the colonel's dacha was no longer in evidence.

"Prepare a report on your findings, a detailed description of this Krivonos and the other man, and leave it with Pankov so I can forward it to the proper parties," said the colonel, clasping his hands before him to show that the conversation and Emil Karpo's investigation had ended.

Karpo understood and rose.

The colonel moved to his desk, sat down behind it, and opened a leather folder the size of a very large book. He took his pen in hand, looked at the contents of the folder, and said, "Enjoy your vacation and return refreshed and prepared to renew your part in our constant vigil against crime."

Emil Karpo left the office, closing the door behind him.

It was slightly after five in the morning. The colonel had said Karpo was to go on vacation tomorrow. Karpo would not disobey a direct order. However, the colonel's order meant that Karpo had all of this day and until midnight of the following day to continue the investigation. If he did not sleep, he had forty-three hours to find Krivonos and the bearded man. In forty-three hours, it would be Thursday.

Karpo wasted no time. He went to the elevator,

aware that people were avoiding his eyes, pretending, as they always did, that they had just remembered something that had to be done in the opposite direction, suddenly saying something urgent and animatedly to whomever they were walking with and giving the companion undivided attention. A woman, who Karpo knew was Amelia Smintpotkov in Records Two, muttered, "Vampire," when she thought she was safely out of Karpo's hearing. Amelia Smintpotkov might well have needed the day off had she known that Karpo heard her and knew her name. In fact, Karpo was unmoved by the reaction to him or by the muttered word. If anything, though he might not be able to admit it to himself, he was mildly pleased. The privileges of police authority were rapidly being taken away. Others around him were finding it frustrating and quite difficult to deal with criminals and a public that were losing their fear of the law. Karpo was confident of his own ability to create fear without recourse to threats or action.

He took the elevator down to the unnumbered laboratory of Boris Kostnitsov, two levels below the ground in Petrovka. Kostnitsov was an assistant director of the MVD laboratory, though he assisted no one and had no contact with the director, whose name he did not know or care to know. Boris Kostnitsov worked alone. He had been assigned an assistant once, but the man had quit after four days, insisting that Kostnitsov was a madman. It was generally agreed that the assistant was right, but it was also agreed that Kostnitsov was brilliant.

Karpo knocked once, firmly, at the gray metal door

of the laboratory and waited. Before opening the door, Kostnitsov's high voice said, "Inspector Karpo. I know that knock."

Then the door opened, and Karpo found himself facing Kostnitsov, a man of no particular distinction, medium height, somewhere in his fifties, a little belly, straight white hair brushed back, bad teeth, and a red face. Kostnitsov was wearing a bloodstained blue laboratory coat. His left hand opened the door so Karpo could step in. His right hand held something white and fleshy about the length of an adult finger.

Kostnitsov pushed the door closed and held up his prize.

"Well?" he asked, head turning just a bit to the side, a knowing hint of a smile on his lips.

"Intestines, small intestines," said Karpo. "Recently removed, human."

Kostnitsov beamed.

"The stomach, the intestines. These are the organs that give the easy answers, that paint the clearest pictures. My favorite organ remains the little-appreciated spleen, but the stomach is the pathologist's friend. That which it contains can reveal much. That which it does not contain can reveal even more. Did you know that each of us eats at least a pound of insects each year? Not the gnat that flies in as we yawn or speak but the bits trapped in drinks, canned foods, meats, fish. And the irony, Comrade, is the pound of insect you eat each year is the most nutritious part of your diet. This intestine. Look. Diseased?" he asked.

"Impossible to determine without close examination," Karpo responded.

Kostnitsov handed the fleshy piece of intestine to Karpo, who took it in his palm and turned it over.

"Discoloration," said Karpo. "Diminution of blood supply. Possibly disease, possibly poison, possibly—"

"Drug," Kostnitsov said, taking his prize back and placing it gently in a white china teacup balanced precariously on top of a pile of thick books towering up from the floor. Dangerously close to the books danced the single flame of a Bunsen burner.

"You got that from the body of the young woman, Carla Wasboniak?"

Kostnitsov moved around his cluttered laboratory tables to his even more cluttered desk and lifted a sheet of paper, which he scanned and put back before making his way back around the tables to Karpo, who waited patiently.

"You want some coffee, tea?" asked Kostnitsov.

"No, thank you, Comrade," said Karpo.

"Why can't they send you down here all the time?" Kostnitsov complained, reaching for the teacup that contained the piece of Carla's intestines and then realizing only at the last instant, as he put it to his lips, that it was not the cup containing tea.

He put the cup down and continued. "Tkach is a child. He poses, and his mind is always somewhere else. That sack Zelach is worthless. Rostnikov, now Rostnikov is not bad, but he has no love of the tangible. The fact is a means, not, as it is to you and me, an end. You understand?"

"I believe so," said Karpo, whose pulsing head told him that precious time was passing. He could, however, do nothing but play out the scene with Kostnitsov or risk losing the man's cooperation. Not even the threat of death could make this man do or say what he did not wish to do or say. Kostnitsov found his teacup and held its charred ceramic bottom over the flame of a Bunsen burner.

"I'll tell you about the bullets first," said Kostnitsov, looking at Karpo. "The ones you brought in."

Karpo said nothing.

"They came from an interesting weapon, West German, adjustable for rapid fire or single action," said Kostnitsov, tasting his tea and deciding that the temperature was acceptable. "The same weapon was used to kill the businessman two weeks ago. German. Special forces, government controlled, but they get out. A Walther RA 2000, but you know that, don't you?"

"Yes," said Karpo.

"Yes. Doesn't matter. The weapon is outside my area of primary concern. The woman died of trauma suffered an instant after contact with the blue-enamel surface of the car she hit. Would you like to know the precise cause of death, the damage to organs from the trauma of impact?"

"If it might be relevant to my investigation," said Karpo. There was no denying it now. The migraine was coming. He would have to work through it. There was no time for retreat to the cool darkness of his small room.

"It is not," said Kostnitsov, tilting his head to the side again, examining Karpo as they spoke and he drank. "However, it may be relevant that the young lady would have been dead in a matter of weeks even had she not been thrown, for she *was* thrown, unless she leaped up and backward through the window."

Kostnitsov juggled his teacup as he turned around and demonstrated the turn. His sloped shoulders lifted, and he went up on his toes like an egg attempting to perform ballet.

"Glass in the shoulders, back of the neck, scalp," he explained.

"She would have been dead in a matter of weeks," Karpo reminded him.

"Ah," Kostnitsov replied, finishing his tea and putting the cup down next to the one containing the intestine, which he now picked up again. "Cocaine with strychnine. Judging from the layers of both substances in the intestines, she had been ingesting increasingly high levels of cocaine mixed with strychnine for several weeks. Even if she took no more, there is enough throughout her body to cause death in two to three weeks. Similar cases, almost undiscovered, took place last year in Paris. Both victims were high-ranking foreign service officers. *French Journal of Pathology*, spring issue last year, had an article."

"Conjecture?" Karpo said as the pulsing on the right side of his head began in earnest. Recently, the headaches had begun to come more frequently and without the warning odors and occasional flashes of light he had experienced since childhood. Now the headaches were suddenly there, without warning, as if his brain were independent, playing a new game with him.

". . . an American association because of the weapon and the drug," Kostnitsov was saying as he now rummaged through one of the drawers of a laboratory table against a wall.

"Please repeat that," Karpo said.

Kostnitsov returned and held out a glass pill bottle containing six blue capsules with yellow dots. The capsules were cushioned by a small wad of cotton on the bottom of the bottle.

"Take one," he said. "That's all I have now. I'll try to get more, but who knows when. Got them from the pocket of a Canadian vacationer who was killed by a drunken cabdriver. Wasted three of them discovering what they were."

"What are they?"

"Something," said Kostnitsov, "that will control your migraine headache so you can function while you do whatever your headache wishes to prevent you from doing."

Karpo looked at the bottle.

A wave of nausea curdled up from his stomach. He opened the bottle, shook out two capsules, and downed them with a gulp. Kostnitsov watched Karpo. The pain did not stop, at least not immediately. The two of them stood for perhaps a minute. First, Karpo's stomach relaxed, and then the throbbing in his head slowed like a steam locomotive coming to a gradual stop.

"I have no more time for this, Inspector," said Kostnitsov, moving back to his desk and searching for something under a mound of coffee-stained journals and papers.

Karpo moved to the door to leave and was taken by an impulse that he did not fully comprehend.

"I will be leaving Moscow for a vacation tomorrow

night," Karpo said, hand on the door, resisting the urge to touch his temples. "Perhaps when I return you can join me for lunch."

"Lunch? Lunch? What day?" asked Kostnitsov without looking up from the sheet of paper he was examining.

"At your convenience," said Karpo, who, in his forty-two years, had never issued an invitation to a meal to anyone.

"Tuesdays are best," casually answered Kostnitsov, who had never, since his mother's death twenty years ago, been asked to join anyone for any meal.

Karpo left.

SIX

The pear-shaped KGB agent with the bald head was Misha Ivanov.

Once it had been made clear that he could not get away with the pretense that he was simply a carpenter on vacation, he had calmly volunteered the information to Rostnikov, who had not looked directly at the man.

Instead, Rostnikov's eyes were on the concertina lady and her captive tourist. Occasionally, Rostnikov would glance at Sarah and the two Americans. The American policeman with the name that sounded Irish or Scotch appeared to be absorbed in the conversation of the two women, but Rostnikov knew his attention was really on him and the bald man.

"You are from Moscow?" asked Rostnikov.

"Yes," said Misha Ivanov, deciding to attack a soggy tart of unknown berries before him.

"I've never seen you."

"Transferred from Odessa two months ago," the man said.

"You are watching me," said Rostnikov.

"Do you wish confirmation? If so, I am unable to give it," said the man.

"The food is not good here," Rostnikov said, looking at the tart.

Misha Ivanov shrugged and kept eating.

"Did you know Georgi Vasilievich?"

"By reputation," said Ivanov. "I saw him with you on several occasions during the past week and obtained identification."

"Do you know he is dead?" Rostnikov asked.

"Yes," Ivanov answered evenly, continuing to eat.

"Did you kill him?" Rostnikov asked.

"No," said Ivanov.

The man was not impressive looking, but he was, Rostnikov had decided, both formidable and professional, which meant it was almost impossible to tell when he was lying.

"He was murdered," Rostnikov said as Ivanov finished his tart and wiped his chin.

"So it would seem," said Ivanov, shaking his head, not for the death of Georgi Vasilievich but the poor quality of the tart, for which he had apparently had great expectations.

For the first time since Rostnikov had sat at the table, Ivanov turned to face him. The bald man's face was white, with red cheeks. There was something of the potential clown in Misha Ivanov, but Rostnikov did not make the mistake of giving in to the facade. Rostnikov had learned that in his professional life there was very little room for mistakes.

"The woman plays the concertina very badly. Perhaps we should meet in the morning," said Ivanov. "For breakfast. The table outside, if weather permits."

"Are you sure you don't want a less observable meeting? The possibility exists that someone is also watching you, Comrade Ivanov."

"A definite possibility," Ivanov said. "I would say a likelihood. If so, I have already been compromised by your sitting here, but I'm sure you have already considered this and come to the same conclusion. May I rise now?"

Rostnikov folded his hands on the table in front of him, and Ivanov rose.

"Tomorrow," said Ivanov. "Shall we say nine?"

"Tomorrow," agreed Rostnikov, rising. "Nine."

The two men did not shake hands. Accompanied by the whine of the concertina, Misha Ivanov left the dining room, and Rostnikov limped back to his table. He decided he would try to reach Emil Karpo early the next morning.

It was just after three when Sasha Tkach awoke in Tamara's bed. He was not sure what woke him, Tamara's snoring, guilt, the uncomfortable lumps in the mattress, but wake he did, and rise he did. Tamara stirred and stopped snoring.

"My little Jew," she moaned sleepily, her eyes closed.

"I must go," he said, finding his underwear and pants.

"No," she groaned, turning on her side. And then: "Later. Tonight."

"Yes," he said. "Tonight," he said, but he meant, No. Never.

She was snoring again before he finished dressing and went for the door. The small apartment smelled sweet, too sweet. If he stayed much longer, he would be ill. Perhaps that was what had awakened him. It was a smell he remembered, associated with someone, a woman from his childhood. It didn't matter. Sasha had no trouble leaving puzzles unfinished.

He went out as quietly as he could into the hall, took a deep breath of the stale but unsweetened air, and found that he had to lean back against the door. His legs were trembling. Stupid, he had been stupid. He should sort out what he did, why he had done it. He knew he would try later and that something within him would distract him.

In a few moments his legs felt a bit stronger, so he took a few steps and touched his face. He would need a shave, a clean shirt, before he packed up the computer and went back to the subway and made his way to the work cubicle of Yon Mandelstem. He dreaded going back to that cubicle. He dreaded going on with his masquerade as computer expert and Jew. And now he would need a lie for Zelach. Since it was Zelach, it would not be difficult.

On the darkened stairwell he could hear the sound of footsteps echoing off the walls. He moved up slowly and almost bumped into a young man in a suit carrying a briefcase and with a cautious look in his dark eyes. They almost collided, and the man let out a sudden "Uhh" of surprise.

"*Prastee't'e.* I'm sorry," the young man said, clutching

his case suddenly to his chest and trying to move past Tkach. One of those unintentional games began. Sasha tried to get out of the man's way by moving left, but the man moved right and was in front of him. Sasha and the man moved in the opposite direction, and a look of panic filled the man's eyes.

It was not that Sasha looked formidable, though it was early, he did need a shave, and his clothes were rumpled. There was certainly a look of anguish on the face of the detective that may well have been taken for something else.

"I have nothing," the young man said in panic, assuming robbery. "Look in my case. Nothing. Just papers."

"No," said Tkach, putting out a hand to touch the man's arm, to reassure him, short of confessing, that he was a policeman.

The man opened the case and held it out for Sasha to see. He was having trouble catching his breath.

"See, nothing," he said with a trace of a sob. "This can't keep happening. I have nowhere to go."

"I'm not a robber," said Tkach. "I live upstairs. I just want to get to my apartment and change for work."

Without another word, the young man closed his briefcase and hurried past Tkach and down the stairwell.

He would shower when he got to the room. It was early, before dawn. Maybe there would be warm water left. It should take no more than a minute or two to give Zelach a story. He would begin by calling him Arkady. No one called Zelach Arkady. Then he would say, "I was followed last night and had to hide." Or, "I followed a suspicious pair of men. Turned out to be nothing."

He was almost at the door when he caught the slightest odor of Tamara's sweetness. It was probably on his clothing. The clothes would have to be cleaned. He didn't want to wear the same clothes when he went home to Maya and the baby. He should throw them away, wanted to throw them away, but he couldn't afford to. He reached for the door to the apartment and decided that if Tamara insisted on pursuing their relationship, he would have to alter the persona he had developed for Yon. Yon would now suggest violence and the possibility that he was more than a little mad, a person to be avoided.

Sasha reached into his pocket for his key but couldn't find it. No, no, no. He had probably dropped it on the floor of Tamara's apartment when she took off his clothes. And that thought reminded him of his glasses, which were also missing. What if she looked through them, saw they were plain glass? He would have to see her, to get the glasses back, to get his key. He had planned to knock gently, identify himself to Zelach and unlock the door. Now he would simply have to knock on the door. He raised his hand to do so and realized that the door was not fully closed.

Thoughts came quickly. Was it possible that he had simply forgotten to close the door completely when he left? No. Zelach had gone out, perhaps to look for him, and accidentally left the door slightly ajar either when he went out or came back. Those were hopes rather than likelihoods. Sasha had no gun, no weapon, or he would have taken it out now as he pushed open the door.

The lights were on.

"Zelach," Tkach said softly, leaving the door open behind him.

The first thing he noticed was that the table across the room was empty, that the computer was missing. He stepped into the room cautiously, being certain no one was behind the door, and then he saw the trail of blood across the linoleum. His eyes followed the trail to Zelach's body, on the floor, halfway into the little bedroom. Zelach was on his stomach, the back of his shirt dark with blood.

And then there was no thought, only action, and Tkach's awareness that he was making sounds, perhaps even speaking but not knowing what he said as he moved quickly to Zelach, knelt at his side, and turned him over. Zelach's left eye was an almost closed purple balloon from which blood curled down his cheek and chin. The chin was split across as if someone had tried to carve a second mouth in the wrong place. The cut was still wet. A thick, almost circular cake of blood with one pod pointing down his forehead lay in Zelach's hair like a recently dead amoeba. Sasha's hands moved quickly from Zelach's neck down, searching for bullet wounds front and back. He found none. That didn't mean there were none, only that they were not in the most dangerous, most obvious places.

Tkach leaned over, touched Zelach's chest, detected beating, and then put the back of his right hand less than an inch below Zelach's nose. He was sure, at least he hoped, that the fine hairs on his hand moved with the faintness of the fallen man's breath.

"Arkady," Sasha whispered, "*eeveenee't'e, pazhaha'lsta.* Please forgive me."

Tkach's next instinct was to call for help, but he was sure no one would come running to help a shouting man in Moscow at three in the morning. He got up, went into the hall, and knocked on the door to the apartment directly across from the one in which he had briefly lived as Yon Mandelstem.

"What?" a man called in a quivering, frightened voice.

"Police. Do you have a phone?"

"Yes, no," came the man's voice.

"Open the door now," said Tkach, knowing that his voice was cracking, "or I will have you charged with obstructing a police officer in the line of duty."

"You are the police?" the man beyond the door said, coming closer.

"Yes," Tkach shouted.

"I am a veteran," the man said, opening the door.

Sasha pushed past the man and had only the impression that he was fragile. He saw the phone and moved to it. He had to hurry, had to get back to Zelach.

With a calmness that amazed and appalled him, Sasha called Petrovka 38 and told the woman who answered to send an ambulance and help. Then he asked to leave a message for Inspector Karpo, to tell him to get to the apartment. The operator paused and then came back on the line.

"Ambulance is on the way. Team dispatched. Inspector Karpo is on vacation."

"Yes," said Tkach, hanging up the phone and hurrying to the door past the fragile man. Rostnikov, too, was on vacation. He would, as he deserved, face this alone.

Zelach emitted a sound, definitely a sound, as Tkach

entered the room and moved quickly to kneel next to him.

"Don't move, Arkady. An ambulance is on the way."

"My gun," Zelach said in near panic, his remaining good eye scanning the ceiling and Sasha's face.

Tkach reached around to Zelach's holster. The gun wasn't there.

"I'll find it," said Tkach. "Don't move."

Zelach was panicked now. He put his right hand behind him to try to sit up, and then his left arm made a spastic movement, and Zelach screamed silently. His mouth opened, tears bubbled in the corner of his good eye, and he sank back on the floor. Sasha caught his head before it struck the hard floor. The sudden movement started Zelach's chin bleeding again.

"Computer," Zelach said, trying to turn his head toward the table. He couldn't do it, but the movement started him coughing, and the coughing brought pain.

"It's gone," said Tkach.

Zelach's eye moved to Tkach's face.

"Crying?"

Tkach didn't answer.

"For me?"

"Who did this?" asked Tkach, but he knew; even before Zelach spoke, he knew.

"Two men, big, one with a yellow beard, long hair. One with red hair. Water. Can I have water?"

"Not now," Sasha said. "You may have injuries inside."

"Dry, thirsty," Zelach said, turning his head from side to side, in search of water.

"Soon," said Tkach. "When did they come?"

"Water would be good," he answered. "*Tkach, oo men-yah' boleet galavah*. My head hurts."

"Water might be very bad."

"Before I could—"

"We'll talk later, Arkady," Tkach said as he heard the first distant blare of the ambulance.

"Later," Zelach agreed. "Yes. You called an ambulance?"

"Yes."

"I heard you call an ambulance. I'm going to the hospital. Tell my mother. Don't frighten her, please. Tell her I'm fine even if I am not."

"I will. I want to tell you what happened last night, why I wasn't here with you."

But the lie didn't come. The ambulance was close now. He could get the lie out, but it would not come.

"I was with a woman. I should have been here, but—"

"You know where I live? You know my number?" Zelach said, closing his good eye.

"I can get it," said Tkach. "Last night . . ."

"Do I look very bad, Sasha?" he said, so softly that Tkach could hardly hear him, and then a man came through the door, and another man, and a woman and an MVD officer whom Tkach recognized, Dolnetzin, the man in charge of the computer-theft squad.

"You do not look good, Arkady," Tkach said.

"Keep my mother away. Lie to her," Zelach said. "I think my eye hurts the most."

Dolnetzin looked down at Zelach, sighed very deeply,

and whispered orders to the man and the woman with him as they went back out through the door.

Sasha was not sure if Zelach had heard his confession or had absorbed it if he had. It had been stupid and self-serving to confess. Zelach was in no condition to ease Sasha's guilt. There would be time later.

"Tkach," said Dolnetzin, a tall young man with a mustache that helped only a little in making him look older. He was no more than a year older than Sasha, but two grades higher and in charge. "What happened?"

"Later," said Tkach, holding Zelach's hand and not looking at Dolnetzin as the ambulance driver and an assistant hurried in with a stretcher.

For now Tkach would not be getting a shower. He would wear the clothing that smelled of Tamara, perhaps for hours, and, he decided, as he stood up, that was as it should be and what he deserved, for he knew that while he had slept in her bed, two men had turned Zelach into the pained creature before him.

The ambulance driver and his assistant opened the stretcher and tried to place Zelach on it carefully, slowly, but even the tiniest movement caused a groan of agony.

Sasha stood and turned to face Dolnetzin, who waited, hands folded in front of him. Dolnetzin wore a British tweed jacket over a white shirt and a plaid sweater.

"I'm going to the hospital with Zelach," Sasha announced.

"What happened?" Dolnetzin asked again, much more firmly than before.

"I failed him," said Sasha, looking anxiously toward the door and seeing the handle of Zelach's gun barely poking out from beneath a reproduction of a seascape that had apparently fallen to the floor in the struggle.

"I will need more than that, Tkach," Dolnetzin said.

"There is no more," said Sasha, moving to the seascape, picking up the weapon, and putting it into his pocket. "Now I must go."

He hurried through the door and ran after the stretcher.

Dolnetzin had twice seen others lose control when they had felt responsible for the death of a fellow officer. There was a madness in their eyes that could either be fought or allowed to run its course. Dolnetzin decided to let it run its course, which was why at such an early age he was a full inspector in charge of a division, with the promise of a very bright future.

Yakov Krivonos was gone. He had been replaced by Yakov Shechedrin. Yakov looked in the mirror at the young man before him. It was the kind of young man he hated. Short hair combed back, perfectly shaved, wearing a suit with a tie.

"Wear these," Jerold said, handing him a pair of glasses with heavy dark rims.

"No," said Yakov.

"Wear them," Jerold said again. "Believe me."

Yakov put on the glasses and looked at himself again in the mirror. No doubt. If he had encountered a person like this yesterday, he would have wanted to hurt him, may even have followed him, beaten him, and taken his money and the watch he was wearing, kicked him two or three times in the face.

"I don't like it," Yakov said.

"One day," said Jerold. "Then you'll be on a plane for Paris. Money and Paris. And then Las Vegas."

"I don't like it," Yakov repeated, looking at himself in the mirror, scowling at himself. He was sure Carla would laugh at him when she saw what he looked like. She would laugh at him in spite of what he would do. She would laugh at him, and he would throw her through the window again. And then he remembered. How could he forget that? Carla was dead. She wasn't going to laugh at him.

Jerold looked over Yakov's shoulder and smiled. "You look fine. No one will notice you. Let's go over it again."

"I know it," said Yakov, turning from the mirror. "I don't have to go over it."

"We go over it one time more, maybe two," said Jerold gently, reasonably, "and then I give you two capsules. No, I'll give you four."

Yakov make it clear that he was annoyed with a surly response of "All right."

And with that Jerold lifted a briefcase onto the table, opened it, and revealed a compact piece of finely polished, smooth maple wood, with a pistol grip on one end, and tubes of metal and a telescopic sight painted black, each piece firmly and neatly held in place by at least two black straps.

Yakov stood in front of the open briefcase and looked at Jerold, who pulled out a stopwatch.

"Twenty seconds last time," said Jerold. "Let's get it

down to eighteen. Fifteen gets you two extra capsules. Now."

Yakov moved quickly. His fingers were too short for playing the guitar, which was what he planned to do—learn to play the guitar and start a rock band in Las Vegas. But Yakov did not have the discipline to play a musical instrument. Jerold helped him, coached him, told him he was talented, assured him that he would make it, that the idea of a Soviet rock bank in Las Vegas would create a sensation. He told Yakov of American girls, and Yakov listened and took the capsules.

"I have an important question," Yakov said in English, his fingers moving to the sections of the Walther WA 2000 in the briefcase. "I have been thinking much about it."

"Yes."

"Does Madonna have real yellow hair?"

"It is real," said Jerold quite seriously.

"You have seen?"

"Yes."

"There," said Yakov, holding the assembled weapon in his hand, the same weapon with which he had shot through the door at Emil Karpo.

"Eighteen seconds," Jerold said, putting the watch down and smiling.

Yakov nodded his head knowingly. He knew he was getting better.

In fact, he was not. Jerold had lied. It had taken Yakov twenty-two seconds. He had lied because he wanted an excuse for giving Yakov the extra capsules, wanted the excuse for bringing Yakov Krivonos closer

to death, as close as he could possibly bring him after
Yakov completed the task that had been set for him
with the weapon he now lovingly cradled in his arms
like a favored stuffed animal.

Not long after Sasha Tkach opened the door to the
apartment in Engels Four, two women in Yalta, sitting
on a park bench, began laughing.

The women had started early in the morning with a
cup of tea just inside the lobby of the Lermontov Hotel.
Had either Sarah Rostnikov or Andy McQuinton had
a better grasp or any real grasp of each other's language,
they might have abandoned the outing. When they had
left the hotel, the sky had been gray and getting darker.
A wind threatened, and the temperature had dropped
to fifty degrees Fahrenheit, but they were formidably
dressed and suitably determined.

They had smiled at each other in the lobby and
exchanged shrugs, indicating the awkwardness of the
situation into which they had been cast the night
before. In spite of that awkwardness, it was clear that
they wanted to share each other's company. It was also
clear that Sarah would take the lead. She knew a little
English compared to Andy's complete lack of Russian.
Besides, it was her country.

What surprised Sarah was that she was the more
physically able of the two. Sarah, who was only weeks
beyond major surgery, was by far the more vigorous,
and in spite of Andy's willingness to go into town on
the bus, it was clear that she was not well.

What they lacked in health, they made up in determination. The bus dropped them at the end of Roosevelt Avenue in Yalta's Old City. The grayness of the early morning gave way to sun and the cold dawn and turned into cool morning. They turned left out of Roosevelt onto Lenin Street, Yalta's main street, which runs along the sea. When they crossed the bridge over the Vodopadnaya River, Andy was slowing noticeably.

When they reached Gagarin Park, just a bit beyond, Andy was breathing heavily. Sarah found a bench near the statue of Gorky, just inside the entrance to the park.

The temperature had climbed to sixty, and robed bathers hurried past them through the park to the nearby beach.

Andy was breathing a bit less heavily. She pointed at the statue and opened her eyes wide.

"Maxim Gorky," Sarah said. "You know?"

"Gorky, writer. Yes," said Andy.

Andy's face was pale and her well-kept hair a bit disheveled.

"Gorky," Sarah said, searching for words in English, "live . . ."

She pointed toward Viokov Street, where Gorky had lived at the turn of the century, just doors away from where Anton Chekhov's school stood. Sarah's plan had been to walk down to the beach, but considering Andy's face, she changed her mind.

The women smiled at each other and watched the determined bathers of all ages head for the cold waters of the Black Sea. A young man with his hair cut quite short and a pretty young woman with long dark hair laughed their way past them.

"He looks a little like my son James," Andy said.

"*Gavaree't'e, pazhaha'lsta, me'dlenn'eye,*" Sarah answered, and then said in English, "Please speak more slow."

"I'm sorry," said Andy. "Wait."

She opened the knit purse resting in her lap, found a leather sheaf of snapshots, and opened it. She handed the photos to Sarah and pointed to the picture of a young man and woman.

"Jim," she said. "My son."

"*Sin,*" said Sarah, reaching into her purse to pull out her wallet. She opened it to a photograph of Iosef, still in his army uniform.

"Handsome," said Andy.

Sarah pointed at the photograph of Jim and said, "Jim, too."

They both laughed, a laughter that would not stop, a laughter they both enjoyed and did not want to let go of, a laughter well beyond the humor of the situation. Tears came and people passed. People smiled and wondered.

The barrier of language had not been bridged. It had been abandoned. They could only sense the potential for warmth or wit in the other that existed beyond language. And their laughter was friendship, and their laughter was frustration.

At the entrance to the park, a small man with one artificial eye listened to the women as he checked his watch and pretended to be waiting for someone. He had followed the women from the hotel and had done so with a dignity of which he was proud, a dignity that did not betray his belief that he had, as always, been given the least important task. Pato—he could not bring himself to think of him as partner—his colleague, had been given the task of following Rostnikov. So be it. There were times when he, Yuri, could demonstrate his determination, take advantage of opportunities to show his skills. It was he who had almost gotten Vasilievich to talk to them, to tell them, not that oaf of a Pato. He had not lost his temper, had not hit the old man, stepped on his fingers, had not killed him, not that he would have hesitated for an instant, not that he wasn't prepared to kill, not that he hadn't been properly— The women were laughing still.

He should get closer. He sighed deeply, looked at his watch again, and tried to give the impression that he was now convinced that the person he pretended to wait for was not coming. With his one good eye watching the two women and his glass eye focused straight ahead, he moved down the path, past the statue of Chekhov and in front of the statue of Gorky, under which the two women sat. He did not hesitate. He moved past them as if he had an appointment. His plan was to find shelter behind trees or a bush, to stay a discreet distance behind. These women were ponderously slow.

"I'll never forget this moment," the skinny American woman said, still laughing as he moved past the bench. He had the distinct impression that they were laughing at him, laughing at his size, his clothes, his misaligned eye, the look on his face.

He could understand no English, had no idea what her words meant. It filled him with frustration, anger, as he headed for a turn in the path behind an outcrop of bushes and wondered if Pato was having a better time than he. He hoped he was not.

*   *   *

At the precise moment the one-eyed man named Yuri passed the two women in Gagarin Park as they sat under the statue of Maxim Gorky, Porfiry Petrovich Rostnikov bit into a sandwich of rough bread, tomatoes, and a rather lumpy butter. He found it quite tasty.

Anton had brought the sandwiches to him and Misha Ivanov on the little rise outside the hotel where Rostnikov and Sarah ate when the weather permitted. Sarah had gone off with the American woman, while the woman's husband remained in their room, saying he welcomed the chance to sleep late for a change. Rostnikov had gone to meet the pear-shaped KGB man, who came out in a heavy denim coat with an artificial fur collar and was definitely overdressed for the rapidly changing weather.

Rostnikov's morning had begun early with two phone calls, one from him to Moscow, the other to him from Moscow.

The first call had come from Sasha Tkach, a rambling confession just before dawn that made little sense to Rostnikov, who had been summoned from his bed to the lobby phone.

"Sasha," Rostnikov had interrupted, "do you know *Alice in Wonderland?*"

"Alice in . . . ? No," Tkach answered.

"You should read it," said Rostnikov. "It is about the Soviet Union. At one point a crazed hat maker says what I am about to say to you: Begin at the beginning and when you come to the end, stop."

Rostnikov had pulled up a nearby chair, tucked in

the unbuttoned shirt he had thrown on over his pants, and sat while Sasha told his tale. When he had finished, Rostnikov said, "Well?"

"I am responsible for what happened to Zelach," he said, unable to keep the anguish from his voice. "I was supposed to be in that apartment, not betraying my wife with a woman I don't know, a woman whose smell I don't like, a woman who—"

"And what would you like to do?" asked Rostnikov, smelling something that might have been coffee brewing in the kitchen. It would probably be quite tasteless, but the odor triggered hope.

"Do? I'm telling you," said Sasha. "You must decide what to do with me."

"Ah, you wish to shift the responsibility to me," said Rostnikov.

"No," said Tkach with some confusion. "I am accepting responsibility. It is your responsibility to judge and punish."

"What would you like me to do?" asked Rostnikov.

"I don't know. That's not my—"

"Shall I tell Colonel Snitkonoy? Demand a review, ask for your dismissal? Shall we call your wife, your mother? Will that make everyone happy? Will you feel better knowing you have made them feel worse? Or will you be relieved of responsibility? No, Sasha, I'm afraid you are going to have to decide what to do. I see nothing to be gained by anyone but you by punishing you. Zelach will not suddenly be cured. The thieves will not suddenly be caught and punished. You want advice? Go sit with Zelach. Call me as soon as you know how he is doing."

"I'm at the hospital," said Sasha. "They say he will live, but he will probably lose the use of his eye."

"Which eye?" asked Rostnikov.

"Which . . . what difference . . . ? The left," said Sasha.

"He will probably need glasses," said Rostnikov. "I think he will look better in glasses, perhaps just a bit more intelligent."

"What shall I do?" asked Tkach.

"You shall suffer," said Rostnikov. "You're Russian. You will suffer. But you will also find the thieves while you suffer. You know where to start?"

"No," said Tkach. "Wait. There's an old woman coming down the hall. I think it must be Zelach's mother. She looks like him. I've got to go."

"Go, and call me back before midnight or after eight tomorrow morning," said Rostnikov. "I like to shave before I answer the phone. And Sasha . . ."

"Yes."

"Survive."

As soon as he hung up the phone, Anton the waiter appeared with a cup of tea and a roll. Rostnikov stood to keep his leg from locking. He took the tea in one hand and the roll in the other.

"It's a scone," said Anton proudly. "British."

Rostnikov bit it and took a sip of tea.

"Tasty," he said, though the roll tasted a bit as Rostnikov imagined crushed seashells might taste.

With a smile of satisfaction, Anton hurried back to the kitchen, and Rostnikov made a call to Moscow. He asked the Petrovka operator to connect him to Emil Karpo's phone. The operator informed him that Inspec-

tor Karpo was out but had left a number where he
could receive messages. Rostnikov recognized the number. He hung up and called it. Mathilde Verson
answered sleepily and with some irritation.

"Yes? What do you want?"

"Rostnikov. Have you ever eaten something called a
British scone?"

"No," she said. Mathilde was also the closest thing,
besides Rostnikov, Emil Karpo had to a friend. Karpo's
relationship to her had been going on for three years.
At first they had met once a month. That increased
to every other Wednesday and now was on an every-
Thursday basis. Rostnikov knew that Karpo was
required to pay Mathilde for each of their encounters.
He also knew that the payment was the mortar that
kept their growing relationship from a situation Karpo
did not wish to handle.

Although she was almost forty, Mathilde lived with
her aunt and cousin on Herzon Street in an apartment
that they vacated in the late afternoon or early evening
so that Mathilde could pursue her profession.

"Scones taste like crushed seashells," Rostnikov told
her, looking at the lump in his hand, "but perhaps I
got a bad one."

"You woke me to tell me that?" she asked with
amusement.

Rostnikov imagined her sitting up in bed, her dark
brown hair loose over her shoulders. Mathilde was not
a pretty woman in the conventional sense, but she was
tall, handsome, strong, confident, and Russian sturdy.

"Karpo," he said.

"Give me your number. I know where to reach him. I'll have him call you right back," she said.

Rostnikov sat watching the bleary-eyed early risers in the lobby as he finished his tea, tore crumbs off his scone, and popped them into his mouth. Emil Karpo was being very careful. Rostnikov knew that if anyone but he had called, Mathilde would have said that she would pass on the message, though she had no idea when she would be hearing from Karpo. Karpo did not want to be reached.

"Call," said the desk clerk across the lobby, and Rostnikov had picked up the phone.

"Emil Karpo," Rostnikov said even before Karpo spoke. "How is Moscow doing without me?"

Although he was accustomed to Rostnikov, Karpo was frequently at a loss in replying to him. Humor was wasted on Karpo, though he recognized it. He recognized but had no idea of how to respond to it. When in doubt, he resorted to literalism.

"Moscow proceeds," he said. "Do you wish to speak?"

Which, Rostnikov knew, meant, did he think this was a safe phone line, one that was not regularly monitored? There was no way of knowing. In fact, it was very likely that the hotel phone was monitored by the KGB. However, it was either no conversation, try to get back to Moscow, or risk the call. Rostnikov decided to take the chance.

"Georgi Vasilievich is dead," said Rostnikov. "He was murdered here yesterday in the morning. An attempt was made to make it look like natural death, a rather unprofessional attempt."

Karpo said nothing. Rostnikov had expected no response. He went on.

"Misha Ivanov, you know him?"

"KGB, recently transferred from Odessa," said Karpo.

"Emil, I doubt if any other member of the MVD in Moscow would know that," said Rostnikov.

"Perhaps," said Karpo.

"He is here, in Yalta," said Rostnikov. "I am wondering how many other KGB, MVD, and GRU investigators are here. Perhaps we could gather for a convention, a dinner."

"You want me to make some inquiries?"

"Do you have the time?"

"I will make the time," said Karpo. "I have been ordered to go on vacation by tomorrow morning."

"To Yalta?" asked Rostnikov.

"No," said Karpo. "Kiev."

"Tell me things, Emil Karpo. Tell me what is going on. Tell me what you are working on."

And Emil Karpo spoke. Concisely, clearly, without interpretation, he told of Carla's death, Yakov Krivonos, and Jerold.

"Conclusions, Emil?" he asked.

"You went on vacation when we were both working on the Bittermunder murder," Karpo said. "Now, as I move close to finding his killer, I am ordered to go on vacation."

"You think someone in authority is protecting this killer with spiked hair?" asked Rostnikov.

"Yes," said Karpo.

"It is possible," Rostnikov agreed. "Perhaps it is a

conspiracy of criminals. Investigators from all over are being sent on vacation to keep them from catching criminals?"

"It does not make sense," said Karpo.

"Indeed it does not," said Rostnikov. "Where are you?"

"A phone near a club, the Billy Joel on Gorky Street. It is owned by a man named Yuri Blin with black market connections, drug connections. Carla Wasboniak came here. So did Yakov."

"A waiter told me last night that the name of Gorky Street has been changed."

"It is my understanding," said Karpo.

"Things are changing quickly. Move softly, Emil Karpo, so that these things do not come loose beneath your feet. Call me when you can."

"I will do so."

Rostnikov had hung up the phone. That had been more than two hours ago.

Now Rostnikov watched as Ivanov ate wordlessly, with massive movements of jaw and sounds that would have offended even the patrons of all but the least savory cafés on what had been Gorky Street.

Anton placed two glasses on the table, each containing a spoon. From the steaming gray pot that he carried in a towel he poured hot water, letting it run down the spoon to keep the water from cracking the glass. The two seated men watched solemnly and continued to eat while Anton put the pot down on the table and, with a flourish, produced a stainless-steel tea holder that he carefully dunked into the two glasses till the liquid in each glass turned a tepid brown.

It wasn't until Anton was safely out of earshot and heading back to the hotel with his cradled pot of water that Rostnikov spoke.

"Are you a reading man, Ivanov?" he asked, reaching for the glass of tea.

Ivanov spoke around the mouthful of sandwich. "I have a passion for English romantics," he said. "And Gothics. Have you heard of Monk Lewis?"

Ivanov's eyes moved to Rostnikov, but the response was a disappointment.

"No," said Porfiry Petrovich.

"Nightmares of the soul," said Ivanov with a movement at the corners of his lips that might have been a smile.

"I will attempt to find a book by Monk Lewis," said Rostnikov.

"I have one with me you can borrow," said Ivanov. "It's in English."

Rostnikov nodded. It did not surprise him that the KGB man knew he read English, nor did it surprise him when Ivanov went on.

"And I will be happy to read one of your American detective romances if you would be kind enough to let me borrow one for a night. I read quickly and with abandon, though I should savor. It is a weakness in me."

A car passed below them on the road, and both men watched it till it was out of sight on its way to town. Then Rostnikov spoke.

"There were many reasons the KGB might follow me."

Ivanov grunted and continued to eat. There was little

left of his sandwich, which, apparently, he devoured with the same zeal he displayed with books.

"But," Rostnikov went on, "they are in the past. Do you like sports, Ivanov?"

Misha Ivanov's sandwich was gone. He brushed his mouth with his left hand and then folded both hands before him on the little table.

"From time to time, particularly hockey, but they are not a passion."

"Do you know why you are watching me?" asked Rostnikov.

"To observe and report," Ivanov said, finding a crumb on the table, picking it up, and popping it into his mouth. "Though I would expect to be relieved today. This is not proper behavior for the two of us."

"And yet . . . ?" Rostnikov urged gently.

"What is it the Americans say? Fuck-shit?" asked Ivanov, now convinced that there were no more crumbs to conquer and sitting back in the chair. "Do you know why I am following you?"

"No," said Porfiry Petrovich. He rolled his glass of rapidly cooling tea between the palms of his thick hands.

"It makes little sense," said Ivanov, unfolding his hands and looking around as if something or someone might suddenly appear and explain the situation to him. "An agent here could have done the job. Between us, we are tripping over each other. One minute I'm arranging security for a visiting delegation from Moscow, and the next minute I'm . . ."

Misha Ivanov looked around and went on. "I do not like the sea air, Rostnikov. I do not see why a ranking officer should be sent a thousand miles to do what any field agent could do. I think *glasnost* is driving men mad."

"Don't you think it a bit dangerous to be saying this to me, Ivanov?" asked Rostnikov, beginning to sense the finest hairs in the tail of an idea.

Misha Ivanov laughed, but there was no mirth in the laughter.

"Even within the KGB there is a new openness," he said, leaning forward and speaking in a whisper that was louder than his voice. "So, do you have an idea?"

"What if," Rostnikov responded, "you were not sent here to watch me?"

"But I was," said Ivanov.

"Perhaps," replied Rostnikov, and for an instant Misha Ivanov considered that he might have been sent to watch a man who was quite possibly going mad.

"And what has this to do with what you said last night? Georgi Vasilievich's death?"

"Murder," Rostnikov amended.

"Murder, then," said Ivanov.

Rostnikov stood. His leg had not only begun the slight electrical tingling that warned him of pain but had gone just a bit beyond. He rose, hoping that he could coax it back to life, make peace with it. He had almost lost himself in pursuit of the tail of that idea.

Ivanov looked up at the barrel of a detective who walked in a small circle.

"There were three of us here," said Rostnikov.

"Three?" echoed Ivanov.

"You, me, Georgi," he said softly. "I wonder if there are more."

Ivanov rose. This was making little sense.

"I'm going to my room to pack," said Ivanov. "Whether I am being watched or not, I will have to report our encounter last night and this morning."

"What do you know of plumbing, Ivanov?"

"Little, less than I know of human nature. Is there a point to your question, Rostnikov?"

"Plumbing is very simple," said Rostnikov. "I have made a study of it. Plumbing always makes sense, is completely logical, and there is a great sense of satisfaction in contributing to its completion. Results are immediate. Function follows form, and there is an end. If it has been done properly . . ."

". . . water flows through the pipes," said Ivanov. "I'm fascinated by this discussion of sewage, Rostnikov."

Anton was heading back toward them now with a tray. Ivanov was torn between waiting to see what food might be on the way and wanting to get away from Rostnikov, about whom he had heard much and in whom he was mightily disappointed.

"You will not be recalled," Rostnikov said. "You will be told to remain here and engage me."

"We shall see," said Ivanov.

Anton had brought a plate of biscuits. Misha Ivanov scooped up a handful and moved away.

"Thank you, Anton," Rostnikov said, reaching over to take a biscuit.

"You have a call from Moscow," Anton said after he had placed the now nearly empty plate on the table. "An Inspector Karpo."

On the way to the phone in the lobby Rostnikov saw the huge man he had seen the day before. The man sat alone, taking up two spaces on an uncomfortable-looking sofa with spindly legs. A newspaper lay open in his lap. Rostnikov wondered where the little man with the glass eye was. For some reason, his absence made Rostnikov uneasy.

SEVEN

Sasha hated the smell of hospital corridors. He had spent many hours, whole nights, in such corridors waiting for victims and violators to survive and speak or to die. He remembered the night when his father had lain dying in a hospital that smelled like this one while he waited all night with his mother.

The waiting wasn't bad. The sound of people in pain was not pleasant, but it was tolerable. What he couldn't stand was the smell and its memories. He always wondered why others did not seem to have the same reaction to the strong, sweet-acrid odor he could actually taste, like shaved metal in his mouth.

But this time Sasha Tkach welcomed the smell, for it overwhelmed the scent of Tamara on his clothes. He was pleased that the smell of the hospital would not be easy for him. Rostnikov had said he would suffer, and suffer within he would, and he also needed something physical to punish his senses as he sat talking to Zelach's mother.

They sat on a bench in the corridor, a long wooden

bench that had been painted pink, probably under the misconception that it would add a touch of color to the grayness. It did not.

Sasha had tried to call Maya. He wanted to see her and Pulcharia, but he was afraid that his clothes, his look, would betray the awful thing he had done and she would be unable to forgive him. Maya had not answered the phone. With each ring he had hoped she would not answer. She had already gone to work. After twenty rings, he had hung up, deeply disappointed that she had not been there, his heart beating wildly. And then he had called Rostnikov. Zelach's mother said something. Sasha apologized and asked her to repeat it.

"He will not die?" Zelach's mother asked for the eleventh time in the past hour.

She was a great lump of a woman, and Sasha could see her son in her.

"He will not die," Sasha reassured her once again, though he had no idea whether Zelach would survive.

"He is my only child," she said softly. "Have I told you that?"

"I knew," said Tkach.

The woman's large nose and eyes were quite red from a constant, slow stream of weeping and nose blowing. She had entered wearing a babushka but had removed it when Tkach had led her to the bench. Her hair had stood up, gone in all directions, wild, ridiculous. She looked like a clown, but Tkach could neither bring himself to tell her nor ignore her.

"Arkady, let me tell you, is not very smart," she said. "I know that. I am not a fool. But he works hard. He does what he is told."

"I know," said Tkach.

"He does what he is told," she repeated, watching a man in white push a cart down the corridor.

"He is a good man," said Tkach.

"He speaks of you fondly," she said, turning to Sasha with a pained smile.

"I . . ." Sasha began, knowing that the confession was about to come out unbidden. He bit it back angrily. Confession, he reminded himself, would be a self-serving indulgence.

Zelach's mother was watching him, waiting for him, with her clown face, to fill out the sentence he had begun. He was rescued by a woman in white who emerged from the surgery, pulling a white surgical mask from her face, and moved toward them. Tkach rose and helped Zelach's mother to her feet.

"He will live," the doctor said wearily with a smile. "I think you should go home now, get some rest, and come back in the morning, when he'll be able to talk."

"Thank you," said Zelach's mother, taking the doctor's hand.

"How is he?" Tkach asked.

"Three broken ribs, one in two places," the doctor said, nodding at a pair of men in suits who hurried past. "Concussion, severely lacerated wound on the chin. The left eye was a problem. He will probably have no vision from it."

"No . . ." the mother began.

"For how long?" asked Tkach.

"For the rest of his life," said the doctor.

"Did he speak?" asked Tkach. "Say anything?"

"One thing, yes," said the doctor, massaging the bridge of her nose. "He said, 'They had a key.' "

Though he now had someplace to go, Sasha had insisted on taking Zelach's mother to her apartment, where she, in turn, had insisted on feeding him a thin fish soup with bread. The idea of food was repellent, and the smell of the fish as he sat was even more threatening than the hospital odor. But he ate, slowly, silently, reassuringly, trying not to think of how tiny the apartment was, how filled it was with photographs of Zelach at all ages, of mementos of the man's life down to a childish framed painting of Borotvitskaya Gate, complete with pyramid tower topped by what looked like an inverted ice cream cone.

"Arkady painted that when he was fourteen," his mother said proudly when Tkach had entered the room and glanced at the less than skillful but certainly recognizable Kremlin tower.

He ate all of the soup, listened to every word, accepted her offer of her son's razor with which to shave, and gave her reassurances and proper responses. It would be over soon, possibly by morning. Zelach would awaken, would tell the investigators what had happened. Tkach had not lied to the team that had come to the hospital, but neither had he told the truth. He had been too distraught, too anxious to go to Petrovka. He was expected to write a full report before the day ended.

"I must go now," he said, turning from the sink in

the corner and handing the old woman the razor he had just rinsed.

The old woman took it.

"This razor was my husband's, Arkady's father's," she said, putting it on an open shelf lined with white paper near the sink. "It was given to him by his captain when the war ended."

"It's very sturdy," said Sasha.

She looked at his freshly shaven face and said, "You are a boy."

He could say nothing, could not even smile. He touched her hand, said, "He will be fine," and hurried out the door.

It was late morning, warm, and the streets were full when Sasha reached the sidewalk. He was filled with a sense of urgency and wondered why he had not felt it before, why he had stumbled through the morning when what he should and must do was quite clear. Perhaps it was too late. He walked quickly, almost ran in the direction of the Engels complex. People stepped out of his way or cursed as he hurried for almost three blocks before he stopped, stood for an instant, and then went to the nearest Metro station.

Twenty minutes later, he was in the clearing beyond the park. He could see the telephone from which he had called Maya the night before. He walked past the bushes where the two men had watched him, along the path where Tamara had walked with her laughing friends.

Sasha was filled with rage as he crossed the concrete square and entered the building. A woman on the stair-

way carrying a cardboard box tied with rope put her
back to the wall to let him pass and then hurried down
the stairs and out the building without looking back.

Sasha ran up the stairs, pushed open the stairwell
door, and moved quickly to the door of the apartment.
He knocked. There was no answer, but he heard someone stir inside.

"Open up," he shouted.

"Who is it?" a man's voice asked.

"Police," he said. "Open the door or I will kick it in."

Sasha knew in his heart that he would not be able to
kick the door down, but if it was not opened very soon,
he would vent his rage upon it.

The door opened. A frightened wisp of a man who
was only as high as Sasha's chest stood before him,
clasping a rumpled blue robe to his bony frame.

"Where is she?"

Sasha pushed the door open and sent the little man
sprawling.

"Who?" the man bleated like a sheep.

Sasha said nothing. The room had been completely
changed in a few hours. Sasha turned his fury on the
little man, who squealed and put his hands up to protect himself.

"Who?" he repeated.

"Tamara," said Sasha, advancing on him.

"Tamara? There's no Tamara here. Oh, the woman,
the noisy one," the man said. "She is below, the apartment below."

Sasha stopped, blood pounding in his head. He was
on the wrong floor.

"I'm sorry," he said, and ran into the hallway.

The door slammed behind him before he had taken two steps. He moved quickly to the stairway and hurried down. Maybe it was too late in the morning. She would be gone, at work. She would have fled. He opened the door to the hallway and moved to the right door. Someone was inside. She was inside. He knocked.

"Yes," she said. "Who is it?"

Sasha opened his mouth to speak, but for an instant he had forgotten the name by which she knew him.

"Me," he said, controlling his voice. "Yon Mandelstem, your little Jew."

"I'm getting ready for work," she said. "I'm late. Come back tonight. Come back at eight."

He could hear her moving away from the door.

"Just for a moment," he said. "I have something for you. I'm late for work, too."

He heard her walk back to the door, and then it opened.

She was wearing a black dress with a thick belt of many colors. Her hair was pulled back, and she was clearly in the process of getting ready. Her face was clear except for the lipstick on her mouth. It gave her a blank look, the look of an android, an unfinished face. She did not look at him but at the large hand mirror she held before her face.

"I look terrible," she said. "But I must go, love. What do you have?"

Sasha was grinning, a wide, awful grin as he pushed past her and closed the door.

"Maybe death," he said, pulling Zelach's gun from his pocket and aiming it at her face.

She backed away from him, looking at him, the red lips of her mime face curled inward in sudden fear.

"What's wrong?" she said. "What's wrong with you?"

He moved toward her, and she backed away till she reached the bed on which they had lain a few hours earlier. She had no room now in which to escape.

"Where are they?"

"They?"

"The two men," he said. "The two men who beat Zelach in my apartment. The two men you work with. The two men you gave my key to."

"Two men?" she said. "I don't know what you're talking about. I'm late for work. I have no time for crazy Jews."

She tried to move past him, tried to show him that in spite of her fear or because of it she was angry and would tolerate no more of his nonsense, even if he had a gun. He grabbed her arm and stopped her. The mirror was in her other hand. She held it like a frying pan and hit Sasha on the forehead. His grip did not loosen.

"The two men," he repeated, tapping the tip of the gun barrel on the edge of the mirror.

She looked into his face and saw madness, and Tamara was afraid. She tightened her grip on the handle of the mirror, ready to hit him again, but he stopped her by saying very softly, "If you hit me again, I will kill you."

And she knew that he meant it. Instead of hitting him with the mirror, she turned it toward him so he could see his face. Blood meandered down from an ugly, raw cut above his right eye, and he saw the look of madness that now made Tamara open her mouth in fear.

"The two men," he said. "I'm a policeman."

"I . . ." she began.

"Do not lie," he said, putting his forehead to hers, whispering his words.

"Now I know why that man was in your room. They told me about it. If you're a policeman, you could get in trouble for what we did last night," she said. "You could lose your job, go to jail. You can't do anything or say anything. Get out of my way."

She tried to pull out of his grasp, but he held tightly and said, "If you do not tell me, I will shoot you, and then I will shoot myself."

He let her pull back enough so that she could see his face again. As she looked at him, he reached down, took the mirror from her hand, and held it up so she could look at her own frightened face, which was now covered with blood from his wound.

"I can't," she said with a sob. "You don't understand."

"You will tell me where they are," he said evenly, forcing her to look into his eyes. "I will get them. You will have enough time to pack whatever you can carry and get out of Moscow. And you will never return to Moscow."

There was no dealing with madness.

She nodded in agreement.

"In the next building," she said. "Engels One. Apartment 304."

Sasha let her go.

"If you call them, I will come back for you," he said, moving to the door.

"I won't call them," she said, reaching up to wipe his blood from her face. "There's no phone here."

Sasha left the apartment.

He encountered no one on the way down the stairs, but outside in the concrete courtyard a quartet of old men parted for him as he strode toward Engels One. The old men looked at Sasha's bloody face, saw the gun in his hand, and hurried on.

Emil Karpo was definitely not good for business at the Billy Joel. It wasn't that business was brisk in the afternoon. On the contrary, most of the tables were empty, and the music was provided by unpaid groups trying out in the hope of a paid nighttime engagement.

Yuri Blin, whose real name was Yuri Tripanskoski, tried to pay no attention to the ghostly figure in black who sat unblinking at a small table near the far wall, watching him. Yuri, who was only twenty-eight but whose great bulk disguised his age, watched the Busted Revolution perform on the slightly raised platform that served as the Billy Joel stage.

Yuri was just developing the proper posture of an overweight, triple-chinned rock impresario. He developed it from watching tapes of American and British gangster movies. The tapes were copies from Finnish television that he bought at 150 American dollars each. Two years ago, Yuri Tripanskoski had been a third-rate black marketeer, a *fartsovschchiki*, dealing in anything he could get his hands on, from Hong Kong cigarette lighters with naked Oriental women painted on them to low-quality duplications of American rock recordings. He had made a poor living and worked much harder than a criminal should have to work. After all, what was the point in engaging in crime if you had to work just as hard and earn just as little as a peasant? But Yuri did what he did. He knew he could not stop.

He had come to Moscow from the Byelorussian town of Gantsevichi, where his father worked on a collective farm. For the first twenty-four years of his life, the greatest excitement he had was a trip to Minsk for a regional party to honor the productivity of the collective on which his father worked. It was during that party, with its tables of food no better than what he got at home, that Yuri decided to change his name and move to Moscow. It took every ruble he had saved and the four hundred he stole from his parents to pay the necessary bribes to get the papers from the local Communist party headquarters.

And in just four years Yuri Blin had moved from petty black marketeer to owner of one of the most popular clubs in Moscow. He was so successful that from time to time he even considered returning the money he had stolen from his parents.

Yuri always wore dark suits and conservative imitation British school ties. He liked to think that he looked like a French businessman.

Perhaps the pale creature in the corner was after a bribe? The threat would come, and Yuri would have to decide. He was already paying bribes to two different groups, the ones in jeans, who called themselves the Mafia, and to the police, who ambled in from time to time in their gray uniforms and red-trimmed caps, playing with their nightsticks.

Yuri could handle them. He had seen Sydney Greenstreet, Francis L. Sullivan, Dan Seymour, Thomas Gomez, Peter Lorre—especially Peter Lorre—handle all of them.

Yuri sat at his table, the table of honor, flanked by Buster and Buddy and watched the Busted Revolution. Yuri had named Buster and Buddy. Their real names were of no concern. They were chosen less for their abilities than their looks. Yuri had cast them carefully. Both men were in their early thirties, and both looked dangerous. Buster was enormous, dark, with a broken nose, hair greased back. Buddy was wiry, albino, with a mean, nervous look. Buster and Buddy wore suits just like Yuri's, but their ties were yellow, with little blue circles. Buster, Buddy, and Yuri were impressive, but the Busted Revolution was not.

The lead singer of the Busted Revolution was a thin boy with long, stringy hair. He wore cutoff jeans and a leather vest and kept losing control of the song he performed, a song he seemed to be creating as he went along. It had started as a version of one of the songs from the Kino album *Night* but had deteriorated into this mess. The backup guitar and the drummer, who wore the same costume as the lead singer, tried to keep up with the lead, but they had neither the talent nor the enthusiasm for it.

Yuri had let them go on too long. The four or five other customers in the place didn't care much. They were treating the Busted Revolution as a joke, but Yuri didn't want them to think he was taking the group seriously. He had only let them go on as long as they had because he did not wish to deal with the pale man in black, though he knew he would have to do so. This was not a regular customer. This was not trade off the street. This was a man with a purpose, and Yuri was in no hurry to discover that purpose, whether bribe or business.

But there was no help for it. The lead singer, who screamed on about *perestroika*, his girlfriend, and Iraq, had strayed into a falsetto that was beyond human tolerance. Yuri removed the cigarette from his lips and leaned over to Buddy, who nodded and shouted over the music, "Stop!"

The drummer and the backup guitar stopped almost instantly. The game was up, and they knew it. The lead, however, who had paid no attention to his band in any case, hit something that resembled a chord and tried to find his way out of a piercing condemnation of the sewage system.

This time Buster stood and bellowed, "Stop!"

And this could not be ignored. The lead singer gave up and looked over at Yuri Blin, who closed his eyes and shook his head no, feeling his chins vibrate, hoping he looked like Francis L. Sullivan in *Night and the City*. Yuri opened his eyes and saw that the Busted Revolution were moving from the small stage as they argued with each other over which of them was responsible for this disaster. Yuri also saw the man in black rise from his table and move toward him.

Buster looked down at the seated Blin for a signal that would tell him how to deal with the advancing man. Yuri put his cigarette back in the corner of his wide mouth, held up a balloon-fingered hand, and gestured in a small, calming motion for Buster to stand quietly and wait. Buddy needed no instruction. He knew his role well.

Emil Karpo stopped in front of the table and looked down at Blin's round, pink face. He paid no attention to either Buster or Buddy.

"I am looking for Yakov Krivonos," Karpo said, holding out his open leather folder, which revealed his MVD identification card.

Yuri Blin barely glanced at the card. He was protected. He paid well to be protected.

"That is not a familiar name," said Blin. "Buster, Buddy, you know anyone named . . . What was that?"

"Yakov Krivonos," said Karpo softly.

Buster and Buddy shook their heads no, but Karpo was not looking at them. His gaze was fixed on Yuri Blin, who looked around the room and sighed.

"I'm sorry, Inspector," said Blin, "but—"

"His hair is orange, in spikes," Karpo said patiently. "He had a girlfriend named Carla Wasboniak."

"I don't know that name, either," said Blin with a smile.

"A pretty blond girl who came in here frequently. She was here last night, at that table. You sat here."

"Sorry," said Blin. "I do not remember. I wish I could help."

Buster shrugged, and Buddy smiled and let out a small squeal of a sound that might have been a laugh.

Karpo blinked once.

"I do not have time for this," he said. "I believe you are lying."

"I am offended," said Blin, now playing to his men.

"You will tell me what you know about Yakov Krivonos and a man, possibly an American, named Jerold."

"I know nothing," said Blin.

Karpo turned away and looked at the people at the other tables. There were not many, and they were all looking back at him. Near the door, the Busted Revolution were packing their drum and guitars and still arguing.

"You will all leave now," said Karpo. "Police business."

At the nearest table were two very young women, possibly still in their teens, and a dark, thin man with graying temples. He looked at Blin for an idea of how to respond. He got no answer. The dark man with graying temples stood up to face Karpo. Their eyes met, and Karpo repeated, "You will all leave now."

The dark, thin man laughed, showing rather bad teeth. He muttered something he was careful to conceal from Karpo and escorted the girls to the door. The remaining few patrons had no teenagers to impress. They left. The lead singer of the Busted Revolution smiled at Karpo and departed with his band.

There were now only the four of them in the Billy Joel, Karpo, Yuri Blin, Buster, and Buddy.

"There are no witnesses," Blin said, looking at Buster and Buddy. "And the word of a policeman is not, I am sorry to say, as important as it was once in such situations, especially when the policeman is dealing with a person with connections. Are you understanding what I am saying?"

In answer, Emil Karpo reached under his jacket and

came out with his pistol. The massive Buster let out a rush of air. Buddy ignored the weapon, folded his arms, and leaned back to see how the policeman would get himself out of the corner he was backing himself into. Karpo placed the weapon on the table, where only he could reach it, and said, "Yakov Krivonos and the man called Jerold."

He got no answer. He expected none at this point.

"Put your left hand on the table, Yuri Tripanskoski."

The smile left Yuri's face when he heard his name, a name he had not heard uttered in more than four years. For an instant, he felt vulnerable, but he rallied quickly, not completely, but quickly.

"What?" he said, looking at Buster and Buddy.

"I do not break the law, Comrade," Karpo said, leaning forward to speak in a near whisper. "I would not ask you to do what I would not do myself in pursuit of crime in the Soviet Union, but I would not hesitate to insist that any citizen do as much as I would do."

Yuri didn't know where this was going, and he didn't like it.

"Yuri?" Buster asked, looking for direction.

"If someone attempts to interfere with an officer investigating an economic or political crime or murder," said Karpo, "I am empowered to stop that interference with whatever force is necessary."

"It's nothing, Buster," Yuri said with a confidence he did not feel and a knowing look at Buddy, who continued to watch.

"Left hand on the table," Karpo said.

Yuri Blin put his fat left hand on the table and felt

the first touches of sweat on his brow. He could neither wipe it away nor admit it.

Karpo's movements were matter-of-fact, efficient without being hurried. With his right hand, he grasped the small finger of his own left hand. His eyes never left those of Yuri Blin, who watched warily, ready to call Buster into play if Karpo pulled a knife from his pocket. But Karpo kept his right hand around his small finger, and Blin wondered if he were about to see some bizarre magic trick.

Karpo bent the little finger back, bent it back until it would bend no more, and then he bent it just a bit more, and a nauseating crack snapped throughout the Billy Joel. Buster went pale and felt as if he were going to pass out. Buddy's arms dropped to his sides, and Yuri Blin felt very sick as he tried to pull his eyes away from the finger that dangled loosely and off to the side. There was silence as Yuri began to hyperventilate.

"You're crazy," said Blin, looking up at Karpo, whose eyes were fixed back upon him. Karpo's face, eyes, showed no pain.

"Where can I find Yakov Krivonos and the man called Jerold?" Karpo said evenly.

Yuri Blin was trembling now. It was a scene he had never wanted to play. He did not want to be Dan Seymour, begging, whimpering, but he could not stop. He said nothing, not because he was determined but because he was too terrified to respond. His eyes went back to the little finger that lolled about.

What if he touches me with that hand? Yuri thought. What if the finger falls off? And, thought Yuri, he shows no pain.

Karpo reached for Yuri Blin's hand with his right hand. Yuri tried to pull back, but Karpo moved too quickly, grasping his wrist, and held him fast.

"Stop him," Yuri said, his mouth prickly dry.

"I will shoot them if they do," said Karpo.

Neither Buster nor Buddy moved as Karpo's fingers crawled to Yuri Blin's little finger and grasped it firmly.

There was nothing to do about it now. Yuri had no control over the little sobs. His chest heaved. His eyes danced. He felt Karpo's fingers tighten on his little finger. Yuri started to pull his hand away, but Karpo had already begun to bend the finger back, and Yuri's movement caused a sudden shock of pain.

It would soon be worse. He knew it. This mad vampire before him would soon break his finger. Then what pain would come?

"You know the apartment building on Kalinin Avenue, the big one behind the Metelista Café?" Blin blurted out, and held his breath, waiting for the awful sound of the crack, the shock of pain.

"Yes," said Karpo.

"They have a place in the apartment building. I don't know where. I don't know what name. I . . . I heard them talking," said Blin. "And I saw this Jerold there, in the outdoor café, under one of the umbrellas."

"You saw him?" Karpo repeated.

"Twice," said Blin, eager now to help, feeling his finger was within a hum of agony. "It's on my way in each morning. Buddy, you've seen him."

"I don't remember," said Buddy.

"Buster?" Yuri asked, almost begging.

"Yes, maybe," Buster said.

Karpo released Yuri Blin's finger. The fat man sank back in his chair, his suit moist with sweat, his eyes turning to Buddy, who looked disappointed.

He wanted to see it happen, thought Yuri Blin. He wanted to see this lunatic break me. He wanted to look into Buddy's eyes, to convey an unmistakable threat, but he couldn't, for he knew that Buddy and Buster had witnessed Yuri Blin breaking. He knew that his relationship with the two would never be the same, and for the first time in his life Yuri Blin seriously considered murder, not the murder of the vampire policeman who had just put his gun away and backed toward the door, but the murder of the men he had created and named Buster and Buddy, the men who had witnessed the total humiliation that Yuri Blin had fled his family to avoid.

"Do not call or try to warn Krivonos," said Karpo, his right hand on the door handle. "Or I will return."

Yuri Blin said nothing. He had no intention of telling Krivonos or the American that he had betrayed them because he was afraid of a broken little finger. Yuri had no doubt that Krivonos or the American would do far worse than break a finger if they knew what he had told this insane policeman.

When Karpo went through the front door of the Billy Joel into the street, he resisted the pain throbbing through his finger, up his arm, and into his elbow, where it felt as if someone were jabbing him with sharp, thick needles of electricity. He walked slowly to the nearest corner, assured himself that he was not followed, and made the turn.

There were people on the street, but they did not

stare at the pale man who grasped the little finger of his left hand, that is, no one stared but a small girl being pulled along by a woman so worn by work and worry that she could have been the child's mother or grandmother. The child stared as she moved past the man and watched him move his finger and grit his teeth. She was disappointed to see that the man had no fangs.

When the girl was past him, she heard a cracking sound and tried to turn to look at the strange man, but the woman pulled her away.

The instant Emil Karpo replaced the finger in its socket, relief came, not total relief but enough so that it would not take all of his concentration to function for what he had to do. There would be a level of pain, but it would be manageable.

Every other time the finger had been dislocated had been an accident. It had begun when Karpo had fallen on his hands during the pursuit of a schoolteacher named Vikovsvitska outside the Turkish baths next door to the Hotel Metropole. That had been six years ago. He had brought Vikovsvitska in and had the finger attended to by one of the staff physicians on call to the Procurator General's Office. Karpo had watched the procedure carefully and with great interest. Since then the finger had twice been dislocated. Once during sex with Mathilde Verson in her aunt's apartment and once when he and Rostnikov had to subdue a madwoman who was convinced that Leonid Brezhnev was the husband who had abandoned her after the war. In both of these instances, Karpo had, as he had just done, relocated the finger himself.

In ten minutes, Karpo was on Kalinin Prospekt.

Karpo went through the underground pedestrian tunnel in front of the Arbat Restaurant, walked past the House of Books, strode by the Oktober movie house, the very theater to which he had followed Carla the night before.

He reached the apartment building five minutes later and began the process of trying to locate the one apartment among more than a thousand in the building in which Jerold and Yakov Krivonos might be staying.

It was possible, Karpo knew, that neither Krivonos nor Jerold had obtained the apartment. It was possible that it belonged to someone they knew or someone they paid to use it. It was not only possible, it was likely, but Karpo went through the motions of checking with the building director, a short man with a sagging belly who wore a workman's cap as he sat at a little desk in his office. The man was of no help and complained about the dwindling lack of respect for the party and the growing number of complaints and threats.

"You are a party member?" the man asked, though he knew the answer because he had seen Karpo's party membership card when he opened his wallet. "It's almost a joke to be a party member," the man complained. "Pretty soon Gorbachev will be quitting the party and all of us who have been loyal will be lined up and shot."

Karpo left while the man was still talking and walked back outside and onto Kalinin Prospekt, where he considered what he might do next. He could attempt to enlist aid from Colonel Snitkonoy, to persuade him to assign the necessary twenty to thirty men to go through the apartment building in search of Yakov and Jerold, but that would mean letting the Wolfhound know that he was pursuing the case. He would surely be told directly to leave Moscow. Besides, there was no guarantee they would find the two, who might already have left.

He checked his watch. He had all this afternoon and night and till midnight the next day. He could spend an hour or two watching the entrance before he began a random round of knocking on doors in the apartment building in the hope of finding someone who could lead him to the right apartment.

Karpo's finger throbbed, but not enough to challenge him or to be ignored. He moved through the people on the broad sidewalk and stood with folded arms under a lamppost. He did not buy a newspaper, nor did he watch the people who moved past him. He ignored the unusually high temperature and the humidity and waited, not an hour or two, but four hours, watching people enter and exit the apartment building. It was at the end of the fourth hour that he saw Jerold emerge and turn to his left.

Jerold did not go far. He found an outdoor table at the Metelista Café, one of the dozen tables covered with multicolored umbrellas to keep out the sun. There was a table close to the street, but Jerold chose one in the back and sat so that he could see the street.

Karpo approached carefully, waited till Jerold had ordered, and moved past one of the low, round yellow pots of summer flowers in front of the café. Karpo wanted to get close. He did not plan to shoot the man.

On the contrary, he needed him to locate Krivonos, but if he had to shoot him, Karpo wanted to do it at close range so that he would not miss and no one in the afternoon crowd would be hurt.

Karpo moved carefully along the row of tables near the street, remaining in the shade of each, ignoring the diners at each table. It took him two minutes to get to the cover of the table nearest the man called Jerold.

Karpo considered the possibility that Krivonos might be joining him, but it seemed unlikely that they would come out separately, that they would exercise such caution while displaying such lack of it. Krivonos would need better cover. With his right hand resting in front of him ready to reach into his holster for his gun, Karpo took the five steps across the rectangular pattern in the concrete and sat across from Jerold, who sipped a cup of coffee as he read a copy of *Pravda* he had pulled from his pocket.

"I've taken the liberty of ordering you tea and a Greek sweet," Jerold said in slightly accented Russian as he put down his cup and folded his newspaper. "I wasn't sure whether you or it would arrive first. I watched you from the window for more than two hours."

"I am here to arrest you for your part in aiding the suspect Yakov Krivonos to leave the scene of a murder," said Karpo. "You are also charged with deadly assault against an officer of the Soviet Socialist Republics, unlawful entrance into the apartment of a Soviet citizen, and assault against that citizen. I need not, according to law, inform you of these charges at this time, but I wish you to know that the crimes of which you will be charged are quite serious and Soviet laws are applicable to all regardless of citizenship."

"In short," said Jerold, rubbing the bristles of his beard with the long finger of his left hand, "you want something from me and you hope to get it by warning me of the consequences of what I have done?"

"Precisely," said Karpo.

"Ah, your tea and sweets," said Jerold. "The service here has improved since economic reform. Now there is capitalist incentive to make money, right, Comrade?"

The question was directed at the young waiter, who placed before Karpo a small cup of tea and a plate on which sat a flaky pastry dripping with what may have been honey.

The waiter smiled and said, "Yes, sir."

"Profits are up with ownership if one owns a profit-making business," said Jerold. "But with profit and ownership come a lack of control. Extortion is the new way of life. Prices rise. The Soviet Union, in the throes of economic reform, can find itself as corrupt as Nigeria. You don't mind my talking economics, do you, Inspector?"

"Krivonos," said Karpo, his right hand on his lap, ready to reach for his weapon.

The waiter moved away.

"Well," Jerold went on, "before capitalistic ownership was introduced by your new leaders, people had a fixed income. It may have been low, but it was guaranteed regardless of hard times, regardless of good times. Granted, there was little incentive to work hard, to please customers and clients, and so we have learned to expect little from each other. But what happens to the shopowner, the farmer who is a sudden capitalist? Where does he sell his goods? Before, the government took care of him. Now he is at the mercy of the market, and often, as in the case of the farmer, there is no one to sell to but the government. You see the problem?"

"I see many problems," Karpo said, lifting the tea to his lips with his left hand, careful not to let his little finger exert pressure, his eyes never leaving the face of Jerold.

"Well, now the government, the consumer, can offer what they wish to the new capitalist," Jerold said. "A liftime of security is gone. Freedom and capitalism bring with them insecurity, and our people have all lived their lives under the secure, though often frugal, protective arms of Mother Russia."

"Our people," said Karpo. "You are a Soviet citizen?"

"I am . . ." and Jerold looked up seriously. "I am an enigma."

"Blin called you," said Karpo.

"No," said Jerold. "His young assistant, Buddy. Buddy's name is really Serge. He no longer wishes to be called Buddy. Buddy is a new Soviet capitalist. He sells his services to the highest bidder. He hopes to find economic security through his disloyalty."

"Krivonos," Karpo said, finishing his tea and putting the cup down gently as a pair of children, a boy and a girl, ran by screaming with what was probably delight.

"And if I don't tell you, you'll break my little finger?" Jerold said, holding up his left hand.

Karpo let his eyes move for just an instant to the raised hand and upraised finger, and he knew that he had made a mistake. Jerold's left hand rested on the table. His right hand was under the table.

"I have a gun in my lap," said Jerold easily. "A 9 mm Webley, very noisy. And I'm sure you now have a weapon in your hand. Do we shoot each other? Do I take a chance and shoot and hope to kill you before you respond? Do you do the same? Of course we can sit till a policeman happens by and you can call to him. I'll then have to shoot you and, if I'm still alive, kill the policeman. In any of the above situations, you will be no closer to Krivonos. Tell me, Inspector, even if it did mean you would get him, would it be worth your life?"

"It is my duty," said Karpo. "If it costs me my life, then I will die in the course of my duty. If I value my life more highly than I value the meaning by which I live, then my life has no meaning."

"Fascinating," said Jerold. "But what if your death serves no purpose? If by living you have the possibility of another opportunity, or opportunities, to serve the state, possibly even to find and apprehend Krivonos?"

"Man is capable of rationalizing any action, even inaction," said Karpo.

"You know your Karl Marx," said Jerold.

"I believe my Karl Marx," said Karpo.

"Emil Karpo," said Jerold earnestly, "put your gun away, get up from this table, go home, pack your bag, and go on vacation."

Before Karpo could answer, Jerold sighed and went on. "But of course you can't get up and walk away or you'll be betraying your life. I admire your dedication, but in this strange new world you are a dodo bird. You will not survive unless you embrace pragmatism, and since you will not, you will not survive."

Karpo anticipated the moment almost perfectly. He fell out of his chair to the left as Jerold fired. The white metal chair clattered to the ground. Jerold stood and fired again. The bullet hit the top of the table. People around them screamed. And Karpo, entangled in the chair, fired awkwardly at Jerold, who had moved into a crouch and was backing away toward the street.

Neither man fired again for a beat. Karpo knew he could not fire again at this distance, that there was too much danger of hitting one of the people running away behind Jerold, who raised his weapon for another shot at Karpo, who rolled to his right, pushing the table at which they had sat and sending it and the umbrella toppling. Jerold was out of time. He turned and ran down Kalinin Prospekt to the curb. Karpo rolled from behind the fallen table and kicked the fallen umbrella away as Jerold got into a dark car that had pulled to the curb.

Karpo could not see the driver clearly, but he could see that it was a young man, a young man with glasses and short hair, and he was sure that it was Yakov Krivonos.

As the car pulled away, hitting the rear of a white Volga waiting in front of it, Karpo ran toward it. But when he reached the street, the dark car was weaving through traffic. Karpo was already moving toward the waiting white Volga that Krivonos had hit when he noticed something on the curb. He paused for an instant only to satisfy himself that it was blood. He had hit Jerold.

The driver of the Volga, a thin, bald man wearing a dark suit, stood at the curb, his keys in his hand, looking at the armed specter advancing on him. The bald man threw down his keys and went down on his knees, covering his eyes with his hands, sure that he was about to die.

It was too late. Traffic had closed in on the street. The rush home had begun. The black car was lost.

"Get up," said Karpo. "I'm a policeman."

He put his gun back into the holster under his jacket and kicked the man's keys back to him. Behind him, Karpo could hear the intentionally unpleasant sound of a police vehicle. There would be no point in walking away. He was well aware that he would be easily identified by his description and that there would be a report about the shooting on the desk of the Wolfhound within the hour. But the colonel was a busy man and might not get to that report for hours.

No, Karpo decided, it would be best to return to Petrovka, quickly prepare his report on the incident, get the information Inspector Rostnikov wanted from the computer, and leave before he was again summoned to see the colonel.

A few things had changed this morning. Jerold was injured. Krivonos had definitely changed his appearance, and Jerold had said enough to make Karpo very anxious to talk again to Porfiry Petrovich Rostnikov.

EIGHT

"And now?" Yakov Krivonos said as he watched the thin woman with stringy hair tear away Jerold's pants.

"Nothing changes," said Jerold, who was lying on his stomach in the position the stringy woman had guided him.

"Nothing changes," Yakov agreed, looking around the room.

The room smelled of medicine and tobacco, and the woman, in a baggy black dress with somber purple circles, did nothing to enliven it. She barely spoke and acted as if Yakov were not even in the room.

Yakov had driven more than twenty miles on the Kashira Highway to Gorki Leninskye and to the small house where the woman who now worked on Jerold's pants had opened the door and ushered them in without a word.

"I need my gun," said Yakov, walking around the small room that had been set up as a surgery. "I need my music. When are you getting me another Madonna?"

"Now you need me," said Jerold as the stringy woman cut away the leg of his pants. "Later, you will have Madonna."

Yakov paused in his wandering about the room to look at the bullet wound in Jerold's right side. He knew it would be worth seeing. The front seat of the car he had stolen was soaked with Jerold's blood, and though Jerold had neither moaned nor complained, his voice had dropped just a bit during the ride, and his breathing was definitely heavy. By the time they had reached this house, Jerold was definitely quite pale.

Jerold's wound was dark and round, big enough to put a finger in. Yakov wondered if Jerold would scream if he suddenly poked his finger into the wound. Would the doctor who displayed no emotion scream if Yakov then licked his bloody finger? These were important questions. Questions that should be in a song, a song Yakov should, would, write. Carla had thought his idea of writing songs was ridiculous. She had never said so, but he knew what she thought. He had wonderful ideas for songs. Maybe he would get a group together quickly and perform at the Billy Joel after he killed Yuri Blin. No, he would be in Las Vegas. It was gone. The question he wanted to put into a song. It was gone. Carla had suggested that he write his ideas in a little notebook. Perhaps he would. When Jerold gave him the money, he would write songs, learn to play the guitar, get the best teacher.

"The bone is not broken," the stringy woman doctor said. She had put on a pair of rubber gloves and probed the wound. Jerold had not uttered a sound.

"I can remove the bullet."

"Remove it," said Jerold, turning on his side to look at her.

"You will need blood," the woman said, moving to a sink in the corner in which she dropped the bloody rubber gloves.

"Then get it," said Jerold.

The woman looked at him and nodded, and then she looked at Yakov.

"I'm going out in the woods to play music on Walther and Blackhawk."

The woman looked at Yakov, who met her eyes. It was Yakov who turned away.

"Blackhawk is in the car," said Yakov, looking around the room for something to touch, something to play with.

Yakov considered the possibility of killing the doctor when she finished working on Jerold, but there were many reasons why he knew he would not. He didn't like the idea of touching this emotionless creature. He was afraid she wouldn't react, would just look at him with disapproval regardless of what he did to her, and maybe, as Carla had done, she would taunt him. That was it. Now he remembered why he had thrown Carla through the window. She had taunted him because he was unable to rouse himself, to keep himself erect. Carla had said it was the pills Jerold was giving him, and Carla had smiled. Carla no longer smiled.

"The one who shot you," said Yakov, looking at himself in a mirror over the sink and trying to recognize the Yakov he knew in that clerk's face he saw. "The one who tried to kill me. I can go back and kill him while she takes care of you."

"Stay here," said Jerold behind him.

"You'll take days, a week to—" Yakov said as the stringy woman left the room.

"I will be up in two hours. Nothing changes. And we do not have to kill the policeman. He is of no importance."

"He shot you," said Yakov, turning away from the mirror. There were sharp instruments here, scalpels. It would be fun to hold one, turn it over, let it catch the light. He had done that before, not so many years before.

"Revenge is meaningless," said Jerold, finding it difficult to hold his head up.

"Someone does something to me, it sits in my chest like clay," said Yakov, pointing to his chest. "I want it out."

"Stop thinking of immediate gratification. Think of living in Las Vegas."

Yakov grunted. He saw no scalpel.

Perhaps he would like to live in Hollywood instead of Las Vegas. That would be nice, too. To be rich anywhere in the United States would be nice. To meet Madonna would be nice, but there was a lump of clay forming in the chest of Yakov Krivonos, and it was slowly molding into the face of the policeman who looked like Death. He did not want to look down at it, but he knew he must.

Jerold's eyes were closed as he lay back on the table, but the doctor was looking at Yakov. He avoided her eyes.

"I'll give you something," she said flatly, moving to a cabinet in the corner and opening it.

"He must be able to function," Jerold said, eyes still closed.

The woman did not answer. She opened the cabinet and removed a bottle, which she opened. The capsules she poured into her palm were red and white. She handed them to Yakov, who gulped them down dry.

Before he could stop himself, Yakov said, "Thank you."

But his mother did not answer.

The call from Emil Karpo came in the afternoon, when Rostnikov and McQuinton, the American, were seated in the lobby of the Lermontov, reading. Rostnikov was reading his badly battered copy of Ed McBain's *Ax* for the seventh time, and the American, Lester McQuinton, was reading the copy of Lawrence Block's *When the Sacred Ginmill Closes* that Porfiry Petrovich had lent him.

Rostnikov had spent almost two hours getting to the weight room at the hospital, working out and making his way back. McQuinton had been standing in the lobby, waiting for lunch to be served, when he returned.

"I can't get used to eating lunch at two," he said. "Women aren't back. Want to join me?"

Rostnikov had accepted, and they had eaten the communal mound of an unidentified rice creation with pieces of meat that was heaped upon their plates and served with a vegetable on the side that looked something like okra.

They spoke English at lunch, and Rostnikov had suggested an afternoon of reading while they waited for their wives to return. McQuinton had readily agreed.

"Andy thinks we should be doing, seeing something all the time," he said. "She wants to cram everything in. She thinks it's a waste to relax here when we can relax at home. You know your friend from last night is watching you again?"

Rostnikov had nodded and sat in a chair near the window. Though he was not the least bit chilled, Rostnikov had also brought a sweater from the room, which he wore buttoned to the neck. He had handed McQuinton the Block book he had brought down from his room after noting that his room had been gently, professionally, searched. Misha Ivanov was seated across the lobby, a newspaper in hand, making no effort to conceal the fact that he was performing his duty. He was watching Rostnikov. Rostnikov had been right. Ivanov had not been relieved of his assignment in spite of his direct contact with Rostnikov.

For Rostnikov, it was an afternoon of waiting. There was nothing to be done until Ivanov approached him. Nothing to be done until Karpo called. Nothing to be done till Sarah and the American woman returned. And, as always, doing nothing was the most difficult job of all for a policeman. It was the task that took the greatest toll, that started the policeman thinking about the pettiness of his superiors, the unfairness of his lot, the boredom that often resulted in failure and waste and guilt for having wasted time. Doing nothing, though it was essential, was the greatest threat to a policeman's stability and sanity.

When the call came from Karpo, Rostnikov excused

himself to McQuinton, coaxed his left leg into near cooperation, and moved across the lobby to the booth, knowing Misha Ivanov was watching him across the room.

"Emil Karpo," he said when Karpo identified himself. "Have you had a busy day?"

Karpo recounted his encounter with Jerold and paused while Rostnikov digested the tale.

"Politics and ideology," said Rostnikov. "Passionate murder, drugs, even madness, are so much easier. In America, the police hardly ever deal with politics and ideology."

"The people in America shoot each other for nothing," said Karpo. "For stepping on gymnasium shoes."

"I didn't say it was better, just easier," Rostnikov replied.

"I have seen the list of investigative officers from all branches who are now on vacation. It was far too long to print out without being questioned, and it is not an unusual number for this time of year. There is an upward-percentage variation of only two percent. I have also noted those who are on vacation in the Yalta region. That, too, is not an unusual number, an upward variation over the past six years of five percent. What is unusual is the rank and profile of those on vacation."

"Enlighten me, Emil Karpo," he said, looking through the little round glass door of the phone booth at Misha Ivanov, who was looking directly back at him.

"An unusually high number of senior investigators in all branches are now on vacation," he said. "Normally, the vacations of senior investigators are staggered. The statistical variation is off by more than eighty percent."

"Do you like computers, Emil Karpo?"

"I find them useful," he said.

"You speak to them well," said Rostnikov.

"I do not speak to them," corrected Karpo. "They provide data based upon programs properly established to retrieve information. The computers at Petrovka, if the individual has proper access coding, are capable of retrieving a great deal of interest."

"It has been said," Rostnikov replied, "that Lenin loved telephones, loved them so much that he covered the desks of his apartment with them and actually had the central Moscow switchboard operator located right outside the office in his apartment."

"Lenin did not love telephones as objects," said Karpo. "He wished to control communication during the postrevolutionary period. It was essential."

"And he could listen to any call in Moscow if he wished," said Rostnikov.

"He could," said Karpo.

"I think we shall speak no more on the telephone," said Rostnikov.

"As you think best, Inspector."

"Be cautious, Emil Karpo."

They hung up, and Rostnikov emerged from the booth, picked up two cups of hot tea, and went back to the chair where the American sat reading, a pair of half glasses perched on his nose.

"I'm going to take a walk," said Rostnikov, handing McQuinton one cup of tea and placing the other on the table near the chair in which Rostnikov had left his book. He took off his sweater and placed it next to the book.

"I'll go with you," said McQuinton, closing the book.

"No, please," countered Rostnikov. "The wives should be returning soon. You can greet them. I won't be long."

"Okay with me," McQuinton said, settling back again.

Rostnikov did not enjoy walking. The stress on his leg was great, and though he had a distance he felt it essential to walk each day for his health, he had passed that mark hours ago.

He began his journey by going to the men's room just off the lobby. Misha Ivanov watched him but did not leave his chair. Rostnikov had intentionally taken the cup of tea for himself and left both his sweater and his open book on the chair next to the American. He wished to give the impression that he was going to the rest room and would be right back.

The rest room was in an alcove next to a door that led to the kitchens. The door was seldom used and probably kept locked, but it was a simple door designed to deter. Rostnikov opened it with his pocketknife and went through it, pushing it closed behind him. Misha Ivanov had no reason to think anything was out of the ordinary. It would take him at least three minutes to become professionally concerned enough to check on Rostnikov.

The kitchen was empty, at least there was no one Rostnikov could see, but a woman somewhere sang a folk song in a quite beautiful voice. It struck Rostnikov that the hotel would be better served having the woman with this voice singing in the dining room than the dreaded concertina lady.

In spite of his reluctant leg, Rostnikov was outside the Lermontov in less than a minute. He did not expect much from his excursion, but it was essential if he were to be able to go on to other things. There were times when he found a song playing in his head or saw the face of a minor movie actor or remembered a book and desperately needed to place the author. At these times he found it almost impossible to function efficiently unless that little piece of unnecessary information could be supplied, preferably by his own recollection.

He had carefully searched Georgi Vasilievich's belongings, his room, and had discovered that the dead GRU man had had no friends in the sanitarium and knew no one but Rostnikov in the town. Vasilievich's room had been searched by whoever killed him, and it did not seem that they had found what they were looking for. What was it? Where, if it existed, had Vasilievich put it?

Rostnikov knew the route Georgi had taken each night back to the sanitarium. If Vasilievich knew he was being followed, might he not hide the treasure? Probably not, but possibly so. Rostnikov followed the route.

The sky was clear, with a tangy breeze from the sea. The sweater he had left on the chair would have been welcome. He wended his way down the path from the hotel, across the road, and into the woods. There were trees, just trees, nothing but trees. If Vasilievich had hidden his treasure in a tree, there was little chance of it being found. He would, Rostnikov was sure, hide it someplace protected from the animals and weather, someplace he could retrieve it quickly.

Porfiry Petrovich's eyes scanned the path as he walked. Far ahead of him he heard the laughter of a man and woman, but he did not see them. From time to time, he paused at a promising tree, a formation of stones. Nothing.

The path turned to the sea, and he followed.

In front of him the sound of the man and woman moved farther away. He came to a clearing on his right, an outcrop of rocks and a rotunda offering a view of both the sea and the castlelike sanitarium in the distance. Rostnikov moved cautiously onto the rotunda platform and stood for a moment watching the waves and a quartet of distant birds hovering over the water. One of the birds suddenly plunged into a wave and disappeared. Rostnikov watched till the bird reappeared on the surface of the water, shook itself, and took off again to join the other three.

It was difficult for Rostnikov to kneel. His leg protested and made the process not only awkward but painful, but he did kneel at the edge of the platform and reach under it, his fingers probing, exploring. He felt nothing and moved a bit farther along. Getting up would not be easy. His fingers touched something under the boards, something soft and alive that scuttled away. He had covered less than half the possible undersurface when his fingers caught the edge of something on the rocks. He had almost missed it. Vasilievich's arms and fingers had been longer than those of Rostnikov. It was something pliable. He strained and grasped the prize as well as he could with two fingers and then coaxed it toward him until he could get a more solid grip on it. And then it was out.

Porfiry Petrovich didn't get a good look at what he had found till he raised himself from the platform slowly, his leg paying the price, with the help of the handrail and fence that ringed the little platform. Only when he was standing did he fully understand that he held a clear plastic zippered pouch inside of which there rested a red plastic-covered notebook about the size of a wallet. He removed the notebook, put it in his back pocket, then folded the plastic pouch into a neat rectangle and plunged it into his front right pocket.

Now it was time to get back. He could examine the book later. Misha Ivanov would know that he had gone somewhere, but there was little he could do about it. Besides, if the book contained what Rostnikov assumed it would contain, he would soon be sharing its contents with the KGB man.

Going back proved to be much more difficult than coming. The primary problems were two. First, there was a slight uphill incline out of the woods. Second, the strain on his leg had taken a great toll. Rostnikov was in need of a warm bath or shower. Most of all, he was in need of a chair in which he could sit.

He continued to move, though he was forced every minute or so to pause, apologize to his aching leg, and promise it better treatment in the future. His leg, old enemy that it was, was not listening.

The woods around him were not silent. Birds fluttered, and the sea waves echoed under the canopy of thickly leaved trees. It was a place he would, given rest, like to take Sarah.

That was the thought on his mind when he became quite suddenly aware that he was not alone on the path.

He knew it even before he made the turn. It was not magic. Perhaps it was a flurry of leaves or a lessening of sound or a vibration on the path that he sensed and didn't turn into sensations, but he knew. There was no turning back and no possibility of running. It could be innocent, a stroller in the afternoon. It could be and might be, but Rostnikov doubted that it was.

He considered quickly hiding the notebook or even throwing it off the trail next to a tree or rock he might recognize later, but the chances of his being able to retrieve it would be slight. Instead, he moved forward slowly and made the turn in the path.

Standing about five yards in front of Porfiry Petrovich, blocking his way, were the two men he had seen in the lobby of the Lermontov, a little man with one eye that looked quite mad and another eye that was definitely made of glass. Behind the little man was the other man, an enormous young man with the body of a large refrigerator.

NINE

Sasha Tkach brushed his hair from his eyes, gripped his gun firmly in his right hand, and knocked on the door with his left. A man's voice answered wearily, "Who is it?"

"District water inspection," replied Tkach. "You have a leak. Water is running into the apartment below."

Behind the door, voices, lowered voices, jousted.

Tkach knocked again.

"We're going to have a flood if I don't get to your pipes," he called.

"*Adnoo'meenoo'too.* Wait a minute," came the man's voice coming closer to the door.

There were many possibilities, all with the same conclusion, Tkach decided. When the door opened and the man saw who stood before him with a gun, realized what was in store, he might reach for a weapon, if he had one. Tkach would then shoot him, and the other man, if he were there. If the man did not reach for a weapon, Tkach would provoke him, frighten him, until he made a move.

Locks clicked and clattered inside the apartment, and the door began to open.

Tkach was looking straight ahead. The first thing he wanted the man to see was his eyes.

The door pulled open, and Tkach found himself facing not another man but a window across the room. His weapon came up, ready, expecting that the man had sensed a trap, had gone to the floor, but even as he raised the gun, he lowered his eyes and saw the child before him.

The girl who had opened the door could not have been more than five, though her wide brown eyes looked much older. She was holding a stuffed white rabbit and looked quite frightened at the sight of the man before her.

"*At'e'ts*. Father," she cried, looking at Sasha's drawn weapon and bloody face.

Behind her, near the window across the room, sat a yellow-bearded man with long hair, one of the two men Tkach had seen the night before, one of the two men who, he was sure, had humiliated him, taken his honor and self-respect, and beaten Zelach. The man wore dark pants and a white shirt with the sleeves rolled up. The shirt was not tucked in, and the man wore no shoes or sox. He dropped the newspaper he was reading and stood up as the little girl hurried to him and buried her face against his leg.

"Who are you? What do you want?" the man asked indignantly, but Sasha could see that the man recognized him.

Tkach aimed the gun at the man's chest and looked

around the crowded room. There were two beds in it and, against one wall, a crib.

"Tamara sent me," Sasha said.

The child was sobbing now and holding both her father's leg and the rabbit crushed against her chest.

"I don't know what you're talking about," said the man, patting the head of the little girl gently. "You're frightening Alanya. Put the gun away."

"I'm a police officer," said Tkach, moving into the room and kicking the door shut behind him.

He scanned the room, his gun in front of him. Satisfied that only the three of them were there, he leveled the barrel once again at the bearded man.

"I've done nothing that—" the man began.

"No lies," said Tkach, holding up the palm of his left hand to stop him as the child wept on. "If you lie, even a small lie, I will shoot you dead before your child."

Even as he said it, Tkach knew that his moment had passed, that he could not kill the man while his daughter clung to him, could probably not even do it if she released him and went running out of the apartment. The child had changed things, brought confusion where there had been such simplicity.

The door flew open behind him, and Tkach whirled and went into a crouch, his gun in two hands, ready to shoot the second man, anxious to shoot the second man, but there was no second man.

"*Maht.* Mother," cried the little girl, releasing her father's leg and running past Sasha to Tamara, who stood in the doorway, panting—Tamara, who had taken the time to finish putting on her makeup.

The girl ran into the arms of Tamara, who picked her up and kissed her face and nose, leaving splashes of lipstick that looked like smears of blood.

"Sit down," said Tkach, motioning to a sofa against the wall with his gun.

Tamara hurried to the sofa.

"You, too," said Tkach to the bearded man.

The man moved to join his wife and daughter. Once again, Tkach kicked the door closed.

"Where's the other one?" he demanded. "And don't tell me he's your son or brother or father."

"He's my friend," said the bearded man as he sat next to his wife, who put her head on his shoulder and continued to hold the child, who sobbed uncontrollably.

"Where?" Tkach demanded.

"Let me explain," the man said. "Please put the gun away. You are frightening Alanya. I have no gun. Please."

"Where is he?" Tkach demanded.

The bearded man sighed and stood again.

"Shoot me," he said. "Take me in the hall and shoot me. I don't care. I can't tell you where he is, who he is. I cannot tell you. I will not tell you. You know what I have?"

With this he pointed to his chest and continued.

"I have two apartments, one where I have a daughter, one where my wife prostitutes herself so we can make a living. You know why I can't make a living? I was a political prisoner. I cannot get work. I can only go through life waiting to die and not working or do what I do."

Tkach was in complete confusion as the man began to pace back and forth before him. And then, from the crib against the wall, came the waking cry of a baby.

"You know what else a man like me has? You know?" he went on as he walked, his angry eyes on Tkach. "I have my word. If I tell you where . . . where the person is you seek, I'll have nothing. Better to die now, here, in dignity."

"Sit down," cried Tkach.

"You're frightening Alanya," the bearded man said. "Your face is all bloody."

"Sit down," Tkach shouted, and the man sat and the child cried and the woman named Tamara closed her eyes and began to rock her little girl.

Now the cries from the crib grew louder.

"You almost killed my partner," Tkach screamed. "He will lose an eye."

"We didn't know he was there," said the bearded man. "We thought you were the only one and you were with—"

The bearded man looked at Tamara, whose eyes were still closed.

"He took us by surprise," the man continued. "We fought, tried to hold him down. We wanted the computer, not trouble. Do we have to talk about this in here? The child."

"Here, now," insisted Tkach.

"We've never hurt anyone before," said the man, putting his head in his hands as if he were very tired. Then his head came up, and Tkach could see that the man's eyes were red.

"You want the truth? We've taken eleven computers,

and we're not the only ones. That's the truth. This is
the only time we have taken one in these buildings,
where we live. It was just too . . . too . . . tempting.
And you want to know where . . . the other man is.
He is home, in pain. Your friend broke his ribs, cracked
a bone in his face. My friend is home with his family,
spitting blood into the toilet. Your computer is there,
inside that cabinet. Now, will you please take me out
of here, away from them?"

The woman named Tamara opened her eyes and
looked at Tkach. The baby in the crib was wailing
now.

"Get the child," Tkach said, and the man moved to
the crib and lifted out an infant that could not have
been more than a few months old.

"We took them only from Jews," Tamara said with
a sniffle, accepting the infant from her husband. "We
thought you were a Jew."

Tkach laughed. He had not expected it, but he
laughed.

"You're not a Jew, are you?" she asked, cuddling the
sobbing baby while the child called Alanya continued
to immerse herself in her mother's right breast.

"The Jews are responsible for all our troubles," said
the man. "They started the whole damn Revolution.
Trotsky, the Jews, and now they're destroying the Revolution with their computers, their conspiracy with
Israel."

"We take computers only from the Jews," Tamara
repeated.

Tkach had controlled his laughter now, and through
his tears he looked at the family on the sofa, the family

that thought it was acceptable to steal computers as long as the computers belonged to Jews.

"Jews have money," said the man. "They can get more computers."

"But," said Tkach, "I am a Jew."

"Then," said the man softly, "we are dead."

The man sat erect, flared his nostrils, and urged his wife and daughter to assume the dignity he sought.

"Then shoot us, Jew, as you've shot thousands before us."

The baby had grown silent in her mother's rocking arms, but the child called Alanya had turned her terrified wide eyes back on the bloody-faced madman who had invaded their apartment. This, Tkach could see in her eyes, was what she had been taught to fear, the monstrous Jew.

Tkach put his gun into his pocket and stood looking down at them.

"Give me your wallet," he said.

The man tilted his head to the side, expecting some torture, some trick, and then he reached into his pocket, pulled out his wallet, and held it up.

"Throw it," said Tkach.

And the man threw it. Tkach caught it, removed the identification card, and threw the wallet back.

"You have a pencil?"

"Yes," said the man.

"Get it out."

The man reached into his pocket and came up with the yellow stub of a gnawed pencil.

Tkach gave the man a telephone number and told

him to write. The man wrote the number and looked up.

"Pack your things and get out of Moscow with your family," Tkach said. "It is the same offer I gave your wife. Call your friend and tell him to get out, too. I will keep your card, and you will tell me where you are going. If you do not inform me of where you are within ten days, I will send out a bulletin, and you will be caught and returned to me. When you call me, I will inform the local police, and they will watch you. If you commit a crime, even a small crime, we will come for you."

The man gave a nasty, knowing grunt.

"You have one hour to be out of here," Tkach said, crossing the room to the cabinet and opening the door. "Two hours to be out of Moscow."

"But where can we . . . ?" Tamara began.

"Two hours," Tkach repeated. "And after the phone call to me when you get wherever you decide to go, I want to hear nothing of you or from you ever again."

Tkach retrieved the computer, which had been placed back in its carrying case. He lifted it in one hand and turned to face the family. There was no gratitude in the face of the bearded man, but there was something there that made Tkach sure that he would have his family at least fifty miles from Moscow within hours.

It took Sasha Tkach less than an hour to get back to the office where he had worked as Yon Mandelstem. He had washed the worst of the blood from his face in a fountain in the park, but he still looked sufficiently forbidding that no one in the Metro had come near him and no one in the office questioned him when he came through the door, strode to the corner desk, placed the computer down, and walked back through the row of desks and out the door to the stairway.

In another twenty minutes he was home, in front of his own door, hands trembling as he took out his key. He had wanted to think of something to say, something to tell Maya, but he could not plan, could not anticipate. Whatever came when he saw her would come. She would see his face and know. There was no doubt about that, but he had to see her.

He opened the door, prepared and unprepared. He imagined that he looked very much like the bearded man when the man had thought Sasha was about to shoot him.

Maya wasn't there.

His first reaction was relief. He would be able to sit, ease into the furniture, the familiarity, prepare, but he could not sit. He could wait no longer. He went back through the door and down the stairs. He had to find them.

He hurried into the street, unsure of which way to go, and then he ran toward the series of small shops two blocks away. He found them almost immediately standing in a line outside a cheese shop, though they did not see him. His need was enormous as he rushed forward and called his wife's name.

The people in line turned to him and watched as he ran forward and embraced Maya, who had turned, surprised to see him, her little smile showing concern. Pulcharia was standing at her side, holding her mother's leg, much as the child Alanya had held her father's leg.

"Sasha?" she asked.

He found the similarity of the scenes so painful that when he tried to speak he could not. Maya stepped out of line and cupped his face in her hands. Pulcharia followed her mother and continued to cling.

"Shh, Sasha, shh," she said to him, avoiding the eyes of those in line who watched.

Whatever it was that had done this to her husband, Maya was not sure she wanted to hear it. Emil Karpo had been trying to reach Sasha for hours, had called many times. Perhaps he had talked to Sasha. Perhaps he had told her husband some awful thing.

"Is it Porfiry Petrovich?" she asked. "Has something happened to him, his wife?"

Tkach could not speak. He shook his head no.

"Is it your mother? My mother?"

Again, no.

"Are you . . . do you have something, something I . . . ?"

He managed to say, "No."

"Then it can't be so terrible. Let's go home," she said, picking up Pulcharia. "We have enough to eat for tonight."

"Yes," he said. "Let's go home."

The little man with the glass eye and neatly trimmed beard took a step toward Porfiry Petrovich on the narrow path and held out his hand. He seemed to be addressing both a nearby tree and Rostnikov when he said, "The book."

Rostnikov considered the situation—the little man

with his outstretched arm, the huge, expressionless man behind him, the impossibility of retreat, and the likelihood that these were the men who had killed Georgi Vasilievich.

"We saw you pick something up under the planks of the rotunda," the little man continued as he moved forward. "Vasilievich's book."

Rostnikov stood his ground.

"I am an inspector in the Moscow MVD," said Rostnikov as the small man moved the hand at his side to his pocket and the huge man behind him took three steps forward.

"We are impressed," said the little man. "Are we impressed, Pato?"

Pato advanced four more steps toward Rostnikov in answer to the question.

The little man with the wild eye went on. "You want to see what's in my pocket? I'll make an exchange. What's in my pocket for what's in your pocket."

"I think not," said Rostnikov.

The huge man was no more than a yard away now. He blocked the sun and sent a shadow over Porfiry Petrovich.

"He thinks not," said the little man. "Pato, he thinks not. Well, I'll show him, anyway."

The little man pulled out a little gun.

"Know what this is?" the little man said, one eye looking down at the gun, the other toward Rostnikov.

"A Pieper 6.35 mm, badly in need of oil," answered Rostnikov. "At least fifty years old. It is as likely to kill you as me if you are foolish enough to fire it."

The big man took over. He brushed past the suddenly deflated little man with the wild eye and said, "Enough."

And then the big man held out his hand, and it was a very big hand. Rostnikov looked at the hand and then the face of the man who blocked out the sun.

"No," said Rostnikov.

The big man, Pato, nodded in understanding. This was business. Pato put his hand on Rostnikov's shoulder.

"Death can be much easier than life," the little man said. "You could have given me the book and had a moment to pray before Pato broke your neck. But maybe you are not a religious man? Maybe you are not one of those new Christians who jump to religion and away from Marxist-Leninism like dirty fleas."

The massive hand was squeezing Rostnikov's shoulder now, pushing the policeman down. Rostnikov reached up, put his hands on the wrist behind the hand, and watched the man's face break into a smile that made it quite clear he was amused by the pathetic effort by the aging little barrel of a man with a lame leg.

The smile lasted for less than the blinking of the eye of a night owl in a birch tree. Rostnikov put his good leg back to support him and wrenched the offending arm from his shoulder. The huge man stepped back one pace, letting the sun hit Rostnikov's face. He looked at his hand and at Rostnikov. Rostnikov could see the little man, now that Pato had backed away.

"Just kill him, then, and take the book," the little man said, looking back over his shoulder. "Someone might come and we'd have to kill them, too."

Pato moved forward, one hand grabbing Rostnikov's

hair, the other going to Rostnikov's throat. Rostnikov drove forward off his right leg and threw his shoulder into Pato's stomach. Rostnikov was off balance for the instant he had to put his weight on his bad leg, but he was accustomed to that instant, had experienced it many times when working with his beloved weights. His right leg found the ground beneath him, and he lifted the massive Pato off the ground. The man's hand released Rostnikov's neck. The creature called Pato growled like an animal and clawed at the back of the washtub of a man for the instant before Porfiry Petrovich threw him to the ground. Pato tumbled awkwardly on his shoulder and landed on his back with a great *woosh* of air.

There was a crack like the breaking of a dry tree branch, and something sizzled past Rostnikov, who moved to the fallen man, who was trying to rise. He knew. The Pieper had not exploded. The little man with one eye was firing. But he only fired once before a voice from somewhere close by very calmly called, "Stop."

The little man turned toward the woods, aiming his pistol but seeing nothing.

"Stop," came the voice again. "Put the gun down or see what it is like to try to plug a very large bullet hole in your chest with one of your scrawny little fingers."

Pato was on one knee now, trying to catch his breath. Rostnikov took hold of his arm and helped him rise. The man swung awkwardly with his free arm and hit Rostnikov solidly in the shoulder. Rostnikov released Pato's arm but immediately drove forward and locked his arms around the man's midsection in a bear hug. Pato struggled to free himself, grunting, churning, cursing, but Rostnikov held tight, lifted him once again from the ground, and squeezed. When he had stopped struggling, Rostnikov let loose, and the huge man fell backward to the ground, his head striking the ground with a thud.

"I would not have thought you could do that," Misha Ivanov said, stepping out of the trees, a pistol aimed at the little man, who had dropped his gun. The deep red light of the sun through the trees glinted on Ivanov's bald head. "I mean, I know you lift weights. You won the Sokolniki Recreation Championship last year."

"The year before," Rostnikov corrected, once more helping the fallen Pato to his feet. The fight was definitely out of the huge man.

"So," said Misha Ivanov with a shrug, "once again the records of the KGB are less than perfect. But in Odessa, in all of the Ukraine for that matter, we do not have priority and our computer network—"

"Pato, I have disdain for you," said the one-eyed man, but Pato was too dazed to register the criticism.

"Do you know who these two are?" asked Misha Ivanov.

"They are the ones who killed Georgi Vasilievich," said Rostnikov, guiding Pato to the little man's side.

"Did you?" Misha Ivanov asked, casually glancing at the little man.

"No," said the little man. "We don't even know who you are talking about. We were just out for a walk when this man attacked us and—"

The bullet from Ivanov's gun made a loud noise, a deep, echoing belch that woke the huge man from his daze and sent the little wild-eyed man spinning.

"You shot me," cried the little man, reaching up to his bleeding shoulder. "You might have killed me."

"I tried to kill you," said Misha, shaking his head. "I haven't had much practice. Our ration of bullets is pitiful. You'd think the KGB had an endless supply. Maybe in Moscow, but in Odessa, Tbilisi? No. I'm sorry. I won't miss this time."

He raised his weapon. The little man looked at Pato for help, but there was none coming from him or from Rostnikov, who knew better than to interfere.

"You want to answer questions, either of you?" asked Ivanov.

"No," said Pato.

Ivanov's gun was now aimed squarely at the little man's chest.

"Yes," cried the little man.

"Be quiet, Yuri," Pato said.

"I'm going to shoot you now," said Ivanov. "I am a very impatient man."

"We killed him," the little man said. "We were told to kill him. We were hired. Actually it was Pato who—"

"Yuri," Pato warned.

"Shut up, bear," Misha said. "Let the man speak and live. Who hired you?"

"My arm is bleeding," bleated Yuri, removing his hand from his arm to show the flow of blood.

"Thank you for informing me," said Misha, stepping forward. "Talk or die."

"This is not fair," cried the little man. "Why aren't

you threatening Pato? Why does everyone think I'm the weak one? Is this fair? I lost an eye. I lost a finger. Look. See. Here. They sewed it back on. I can't bend it. Why shoot me?"

"Who hired you?" asked Ivanov.

"The man at the hotel," said Yuri. "At the Lermontov."

Before either Rostnikov or Ivanov could react, the huge man had grabbed the neck of the wild-eyed little man and twisted it with a terrible crack. Ivanov fired three times. The first bullet hit Pato in the neck. The second tore into the right side of his forehead as he spun around, and the third hit him low in the stomach. He dropped the little man, pitched forward on his face silently, and died.

Ivanov and Rostnikov moved forward to the fallen little man, who looked very much like a scrawny dying bird as he lay on his back.

Ivanov kicked the dead Pato once and lifted his head to be sure he was dead. Rostnikov knelt at the side of the little man.

"Don't move," said Rostnikov.

"Can't move," the man whispered, a trail of blood coming out of the corner of his mouth. "Can't feel."

"Who hired you, Yuri?" said Rostnikov gently.

Ivanov, who had joined Rostnikov, hovered over the dying man, his weapon leveled at Yuri's head.

"Answer the man," he said.

"Shoot me," whispered Yuri, his voice fluttering.

"Pato has killed you, Yuri," said Rostnikov. "He has betrayed you."

"Pato was always my friend till he killed me," Yuri breathed, his eyes closing.

"Was it the waiter?" asked Ivanov. "Anton, the waiter?"

"No," said Rostnikov. "It was McQuinton."

"The American. Yes," said Yuri, opening his eyes. The good one found Rostnikov. The glass one looked into forever, and Yuri died.

TEN

There had been no time to confess to Maya.

When they reached the apartment, she had put Pulcharia in her crib for a nap and then helped Sasha cleanse the wound on his head.

"You should go to the clinic," she said. "I think it needs stitches."

But she made it a suggestion, not a demand. There was something more important going on than concern over a physical scar.

"Zelach is in the hospital," he said as she cut away a small patch of his hair so she could close and tape the wound. "He may lose an eye."

"I'm sorry," Maya said with more concern for her husband's anguish than for what had happened to his partner. Maya had met Zelach only twice, and both times very briefly. What little her husband had said about the man had not been particularly complimentary, but the effect of what had happened was clear in the vacant pain in her husband's face. For the first time since she had met him, he looked every day of his age and perhaps even more.

"I must tell you, Maya," he said. "It was my fault."

Maya considered asking him to take his clothes off and get into bed with her. Pulcharia was sleeping. He obviously had some time, and they had not been together for days. Maya was in her fourth month, and the roundness of her tummy was just beginning. When she was carrying Pulcharia, she and Sasha had made love right to the final month, the few times they were able, when Sasha's mother was not in the next room.

Now that they had their own apartment they made love about as frequently as they had when Lydia was around, but they did it with a sense of freedom. But Maya was certain that if she suggested that they now take off their clothes and get in bed, he would reject the idea.

The phone rang. There were two small rooms in the apartment. One was the bedroom with their bed and Pulcharia's. The other was the combination living room and kitchen in which they now sat near the small sink. In the next room the baby stirred, and Maya dashed across the room to answer the phone before it rang again.

Something in her dash, the swish of her dress, stirred a memory within Sasha and made him want to weep.

"It's Karpo," Maya said, holding out the phone to him.

Sasha's knees felt weak beneath him, but he rose and took the phone.

"Yes," said Sasha, looking at Maya, who had crossed back to the sink to clean up.

"Can you be in front of your apartment in three minutes?"

"Three . . . but . . ."

"I am unable to call anyone else," said Karpo. "I am not supposed to be in Moscow. I will explain if you can come. If you cannot, let us terminate this conversation."

"I'll be down in three minutes," Sasha said, and hung up the phone.

Maya looked at him. She was framed against the window. She looked soft, round, and her voice was gentle, with that slight touch of Georgia that always stirred him.

"You are in no condition to do anything or go anywhere, Sasha," she said. But she spoke knowing that he was going, even considering that it might be best for him to go rather than say what he planned to say, for surely now, though he felt the need to speak, she did not feel the need to hear.

"I . . . it will be. I'll be back as soon as I can," he said.

She stepped forward and put her arms around him, her belly against his, and he felt or imagined he felt the baby kick.

"Have you eaten anything today?" she asked, stepping back to look at his face.

"No," he said.

Maya went to the cabinet and took a piece of bread from the enamel bread box with the little flowers, a wedding gift from her mother.

"Thank you," he said, holding the bread in two hands as if it were a precious gift.

"Sasha, it's just a piece of bread."

"I'll stop and see Arkady before I come home," he said, moving to the door.

For a moment she didn't know who her husband was talking about, but then she realized it must be Zelach. She had never before heard his first name.

It was the city of Chekhov, so Rostnikov decided to stage the scene as if it were the end of the second act of one of the master's plays. Misha Ivanov had arranged for the quiet removal from the woods of the bodies of both Pato and Yuri and, after they examined the contents of the notebook Rostnikov had removed from under the rotunda, had agreed to Rostnikov's proposal to stage the scene.

The notebook had contained a list of names and notations. Some of the names had lines through them, others had notes after them, and neatly penned speculations were at the bottom of almost every sheet.

"How many do you count?" Ivanov had said as they sat on a bench near the entrance to the woods. From the bench they could watch the nearby traffic on the road and look up the hill toward the Lermontov Hotel. A gray van was parked no more than ten feet from them, partly blocking their view of the road toward town.

"In Yalta?" Rostnikov answered. "Seventeen. That includes both you, me, and Georgi himself."

"Conspiracy?" asked Ivanov, pulling his jacket around him, though Rostnikov felt no surge of cold air.

"That was clearly Vasilievich's belief," said Rostnikov.

"Confirmed by his death and the interest of those two to obtain this book," said Ivanov.

As he said "those two," the body of Pato was being carried past them on a stretcher by two men, who strained under the weight.

"Something is going to happen in Moscow," said Rostnikov.

Ivanov sighed deeply in answer.

"If Vasilievich was correct, the senior investigators from all branches, KGB, MVD, GRU, who would be most likely to uncover and disrupt this thing, were sent on vacation away from Moscow at the same time."

"Or," added Ivanov, "sent on the pretext of watching one of the investigators. And who knows how many were sent places other than Yalta. When will it happen?"

Rostnikov looked at the notebook.

"Soon, very soon. According to Vasilievich, five of these vacations end the day after tomorrow."

"All right," said Ivanov, standing and brushing fallen leaves from his lap. "The American."

"Yes," said Rostnikov, also rising as the two men took their now empty stretcher back into the woods for the second body.

And that had led them to the scene that Porfiry Petrovich was now playing out with the American. Rostnikov had gone to his room and knocked, and McQuinton had answered, a book in his hand, fully dressed. His white hair was brushed back, but he needed a shave. Little white bristles caught the dim light of the hall.

"Have the women returned?" Rostnikov said.

"Haven't seen them," said McQuinton. "You all right? You look a little—"

"I am, a bit, what is the word? Is it 'disgruntled'?"

"Probably not," said McQuinton. "You want to come in?"

"Yes, thank you."

McQuinton stepped back. Rostnikov entered, and the American closed the door behind him.

"Not much room," said McQuinton, looking at the bed, wooden cabinet, and single straight-backed chair. "Take the chair. Mind if I shave?"

"Thank you," said Rostnikov, "but I would prefer to stand. My leg is misbehaving a bit."

"Suit yourself," said McQuinton, moving to the washroom.

Rostnikov followed him and watched from outside the door. There wasn't enough room inside for two people.

McQuinton ran the water and found his razors in a leather case.

"Damned water never gets warm," he said, wrapping a towel around his neck and patting his face.

"What are those?" asked Rostnikov.

"Disposable razors. Here, take a couple. I brought plenty from the States."

He handed three blue-handled plastic razors to Rostnikov, who put them in his jacket pocket.

"Thank you," he said. "And I have something for you, but it is less in the form of a gift than a burden."

McQuinton was examining himself in the small mirror over the sink as he shaved. Rostnikov removed Vasilievich's notebook from his pocket and held it up where

McQuinton could see it in the mirror. The American's hand did not waver. The stroke from neck to chin was smooth.

"What is it?" he asked.

"A notebook," said Rostnikov.

"What do you want me to do with this burden?" asked McQuinton, turning his head to one side to inspect the progress of his effort. He seemed satisfied.

"Take it with you," said Rostnikov. "Turn it over to the CIA when your plane refuels in Paris."

McQuinton removed the towel from his neck, wiped the remaining soap from his face with it, examined himself in the mirror once more, and turned to face Rostnikov.

"What is it?"

"It contains a list of names of senior Soviet investigators," said Rostnikov. "It documents their ordered departure from Moscow and includes speculation by the senior investigator who compiled the list that all of these men were ordered to take vacations at the same time. It was his belief that something was about to take place in Moscow, something that some high-ranking figures do not want to be stopped by anyone who might be capable of determining what was taking place."

McQuinton looked at Rostnikov and the book and moved out of the small bathroom and to the bed, where he propped up the two pillows and sat against them.

"I don't follow," said the American.

"If something does take place within that period," Rostnikov went on, facing the lounging but attentive American, "this notebook will be evidence that a conspiracy exists."

"And you want me to smuggle the notebook out of the country and turn it over to the CIA? Why?"

"You are leaving. It is possible the CIA will be able to use channels to stop the event, to expose it. If not, they can reveal that the event, which might be made to look like an individual—"

"Rostnikov," said the American. "Spit it out."

"I don't—"

"What's going on?"

"I think an attempt will be made to kill Mikhail Gorbachev within the next two days," said Rostnikov, looking at the notebook. "I think it will be made to look not like a coup from within but a random mad act, probably from a foreigner."

"Holy Christ," said McQuinton, sitting up. "You're not kidding."

"I am not kidding," said Rostnikov.

"Why can't you just take this book to Moscow?"

"I can," said Rostnikov. "I may or may not be believed. I may or may not be allowed to live long enough to air my suspicions. My credibility as an investigator is secure, but my relationship to the KGB, which would have jurisdiction, is weak, and I am not sure which elements of the KGB might be involved. I am being frank with you."

"I appreciate that," said McQuinton, getting off the bed and starting to pace around the room. "But, hell. I'm on vacation with a sick wife. I'm not sure I can risk getting caught with this thing."

"I appreciate your concern," said Rostnikov. "If you would rather not, I fully understand."

"Hold it. I didn't say I wouldn't. Okay." The sigh

was enormous, as if the American were about to take on the responsibilities of the world. He held out his hand for the book.

"You should know that the man who wrote this notebook is dead," said Rostnikov.

"I'm in," said McQuinton, shaking his head.

"Would you like to know who killed him?" Rostnikov asked.

"Yes, it might help cover my ass."

"You killed him," said Rostnikov.

McQuinton's hand wavered inches away from the notebook that Rostnikov held out. Several possibilities went through Lester McQuinton's mind. All were evident in a series of looks that quickly crossed his face. He considered a smile, an assertion that the idea was absurd. He considered violence, a grab for the book and an attempt to overpower and possibly kill Porfiry Petrovich. He may even have considered the possibility of simply running, for Rostnikov could certainly not follow, but where would he run, and besides . . .

Rostnikov had moved to the door, which he opened. Misha Ivanov was standing in the hall, his hands folded in front of him. He stepped into the room, and Rostnikov closed the door.

McQuinton shook his head and sat heavily on the bed.

"Andy really likes your wife," McQuinton said, looking up at Rostnikov. "Hell, what difference does that make, right?"

"Sarah likes your wife also," said Rostnikov. "She is not . . . ?"

"No," said the American. "As far as she knows, we're

just here on a vacation. I saved the money, and here we are."

"My English is terrible, Rostnikov," Misha Ivanov said in Russian. "Ask him."

"Are you an American?" Rostnikov asked, moving back to lean against the low wooden cabinet.

"I'm an American. I'm a cop. No lies. That's about all you get from me unless we deal," said McQuinton.

Rostnikov translated for Ivanov, who said, "Tell him we make no deals."

"Gentlemen," said McQuinton, "I'm an American tourist. I don't know what you've got or think you've got on me, but accusing an American of killing Soviet citizens isn't going to do relations between our countries very much good."

"We both heard Yuri identify you as the man who hired him and Pato to kill Georgi Vasilievich," said Rostnikov. "He and the man called Pato are quite willing to confess both to the murder itself and your responsibility."

"Come on. No motive, no evidence," said McQuinton, but he did not say it with confidence.

"Motive?" asked Rostnikov.

"Reason to want your Vasilievich killed. Did I pronounce the name right?"

"What is he saying?" asked Misha Ivanov impatiently.

"We have no motive, no evidence," Porfiry Petrovich said.

"Tell him I'll shoot him in the face if he doesn't talk," said Ivanov, opening his jacket and pulling out his gun.

Lester McQuinton looked at it but showed no sign of being frightened.

"No, I have a better idea," Misha Ivanov said brightly. "Tell him I will shoot his wife and then I will shoot him."

"Ivanov," Rostnikov said softly, looking at the KGB man, but Rostnikov could see in the man's gentle grin that he meant what he said.

"Tell him," Ivanov insisted.

"He's threatening Andy, isn't he?" McQuinton said.

"Yes," Rostnikov confirmed. "But I would not let him do that."

"You might not be able to stop him," McQuinton said with a sigh. "Good guys and bad guys. Hell. Let's work a deal here. I tell you what I know, you let me get on the plane tonight and go home with my wife. If you think I'm holding back or lying, you arrest me, shoot my ass, or whatever you guys do."

"You would trust us?" asked Rostnikov.

Lester McQuinton ran his thick right hand through his white hair. "I got a choice?"

"Rostnikov, I grow weary," said Ivanov.

Rostnikov explained what McQuinton had said.

"Make the agreement, Porfiry Petrovich," said Misha.

"We honor it," Rostnikov said.

"And we decide if he should be arrested when he is finished," Ivanov said.

Rostnikov nodded at McQuinton.

"I want this done one way or the other before Andy and your wife get back."

"Then speak quickly," said Rostnikov.

"I go to this bar back home," said McQuinton. "Place on Fiftieth Street called On the Way Home."

"I don't . . ." Rostnikov began.

"Bars back home sometimes have these cute names. Idea is that you can call your wife and say you're On the Way Home."

"And that is humorous?"

"Some think so," said McQuinton. "I could use a drink now. Just a beer. Beer in your country stinks."

"I thought you wanted to get this told quickly," said Rostnikov.

And McQuinton changed modes. He spoke quickly and clearly. He was suddenly a policeman, and he gave a policeman's report.

"Guy in this bar got friendly with me, other cops," he said. "Asked questions, said he used to be a cop in Russia. Accent was right, but he didn't look like a cop, not a cop like me or you two. I thought he was full of shit, but he bought drinks. Long story short. One night I told this guy, said his name was Oleg, that Andy was sick and I was broke and getting close to retirement, that I hadn't saved anything and that the pension wouldn't cover . . . You know. Cop grousing."

"Yes," said Rostnikov. He translated the essence to Misha and nodded for McQuinton to go on.

"Oleg says, 'What if?' You know. What if someone handed me fifty thousand dollars. Cash. Tax-free. Plus a free trip to Russia. What would I do for that? I still thought he was full of shit. I said I'd kill for it. Few nights later Oleg came back with the same thing. I said I didn't find it funny anymore. He handed me a package. I figured it was a setup, Internal Affairs. I gave it back and told him to follow me into the john."

"John?"

"Toilet. I checked him out for wires. None. I

checked the john. Clear. I told him to open the envelope. He did. It was full of bills. I still wasn't buying
it, but I wanted to. I made him take out the bills, wipe
'em clean with his handkerchief, and lay 'em on the
sink. When he reached ten thousand dollars, he had my
interest. You know what's crazy? I stopped smoking
twenty years ago. It'd kill me if I started again, but I
need a cigarette now. Crazy."

Rostnikov translated. Misha nodded and pulled out a
pack of cigarettes, which he handed to McQuinton,
who took one, accepted a light from Ivanov, and inhaled
deeply.

"Tastes like I never stopped," McQuinton said, and
then he coughed, a terrible cough. He looked at the
cigarette as the coughing subsided and continued to
smoke as he talked.

"Oleg told me I could take what he had with him and
get the rest before we left the States. He would trust me.
And he said it was possible I might get to keep the money
and not do anything for it. But if anyone approached me
and gave me the right word, I was to do what he told
me. Oleg said I wouldn't have to kill anyone myself, just
call a number and some guys would come. And I'd give
these guys the name of the guy to hit. Like I said before,
sounded like bullshit, but the money was real, and Andy
ain't well, and it wouldn't be the first crap I pulled.
Thirty years a cop is a long time."

Once again, McQuinton paused and smoked while
Rostnikov translated and Ivanov responded.

"The man who approached you?" Rostnikov prodded.

"Woman," corrected McQuinton. "About forty,
plain, dark suit. In the lobby when we got to the hotel

here. Haven't seen her since. She said she had been sent to see me by St. John the Baptist. That was it. She gave me a name and a phone number and said I should tell the guys I hired that the hit might have notes or a book. They were to bring the notes to me. Woman said the money would be in my room under the bed. It was. You saw the two I hired. Fifth-rate. Amateurs, and bad ones at that. That's the story."

McQuinton finished his cigarette, crushed the butt in an ashtray on the table near the bed, and said, "Got to remember to clean that before Andy shows up."

Misha Ivanov heard the rest of McQuinton's tale from Rostnikov and rubbed the tip of his nose gently.

"It's a ridiculous story," Ivanov said, looking at the American. "Why would anyone go through the trouble of hiring an American to do this? Why not do it themselves? It makes no sense."

"You think he is lying?" asked Rostnikov.

"No," said Ivanov. "Conclusion?"

"He's a scapegoat," said Rostnikov. "If this were discovered, as it has been, someone wanted an American blamed. I think Lester McQuinton is fortunate that we got to him before he conveniently had an accident."

"Or conveniently committed suicide," said Ivanov.

There was no knock at the door. It came open, and Misha Ivanov turned toward it, gun in hand.

Andy McQuinton was in the middle of a laugh when she saw the gun. Behind her, Sarah Rostnikov, who had not seen the weapon, was still laughing, but when Andy went silent, she knew something was wrong.

Ivanov put the gun away and moved to close the door behind Sarah as she and Andy stepped in.

"Lester?" the frail woman asked, looking at her husband, who had definitely changed quite a bit in the few hours since she had gone out.

Lester sat up at the edge of the bed.

"Cop talk," said Lester. "Man here's a KGB officer. Showing me his weapon."

"I am sorry," said Misha Ivanov in English with a smile.

Sarah looked at Porfiry Petrovich and knew, not the details, but she knew that something was very wrong in this room. Andy McQuinton was carrying a small package. She put it on the bed and moved to her husband, who took her hand and gave her a false wink of confidence. The frail woman's nose crinkled, and she looked at the dirty ashtray.

"Lester?" she repeated gently, afraid.

"Later, Andy," he said softly.

"Let us go, Misha," said Rostnikov. "The McQuintons have packing to do. There is a plane for Paris in two hours. Perhaps we can all drive them to the airport and sit with them till they leave."

Ivanov looked at the Americans and shook his head a few times before heading for the door. Sarah moved to Andy's side and put her hand on the little woman's shoulder. Without looking back at her, Andy McQuinton touched Sarah's hand. The strong man on the bed was now quite weak, and the weak woman who stood before him had found within her a great strength.

When they had gone into the hall and left the Americans to their packing, Ivanov turned to Rostnikov. Sarah took her husband's hand.

"All right," said Ivanov. "We get them on the plane and then . . ."

"I fly to Moscow and give this book to my division commander," said Rostnikov.

"And he will believe you?"

"He will believe me," said Rostnikov, looking at his wife, who was quite pale.

"And he will act?"

"I do not know," said Rostnikov.

"Porfiry Petrovich, I think we have stepped into something deep and very dirty. I'll arrange for a flight for you tonight. Get ready. I'll wait here till the Americans are prepared to go."

Sarah had not said a word, and she did not do so even when they were back in their room.

"Sarah," he said. "I won't even pack. I'll change clothes at home in Moscow and be back here tomorrow, the next day at the latest."

Sarah Rostnikov was sitting on the chair in the corner.

"Are you all right?" he asked, moving to her side. "Do you have a headache? You want your medication?"

"It follows you wherever you go, Porfiry Petrovich," she said, looking at him.

"Yes," he admitted.

"It is not an accident, is it?"

He was not sure what she meant, but he answered what he understood.

"I do not think so."

"I like the American woman," said Sarah.

"So do I," said Rostnikov.

ELEVEN

They drove in silence. Karpo explained nothing, and
Tkach asked nothing. Neither man was uncomfortable
with the situation, though Emil Karpo noted the lack
of curiosity in his colleague, the wound on his forehead,
and the semidrugged look in his eyes. And these made
Emil Karpo wonder why Rostnikov had told him to
pick up Sasha Tkach before he went in search of Jerold
and Yakov.

He had called Rostnikov about twenty minutes before
he went to Tkach's house. Rostnikov had told him three
things. The first was quite clear, that Zelach had been
injured and that Tkach felt responsible. The second
was quite cryptic, that Rostnikov had run into Karpo's
Uncle Vetz, the uncle they had last seen where they
caught the car thief. Third, Rostnikov said that Sarah
had not been feeling well and was taking naps every
morning at nine. Karpo had expressed concern and
hung up understanding that Inspector Rostnikov had
reason to believe their conversation was listened to and
that Karpo was to be at a specific place at nine the next

morning, the place where he and Rostnikov had caught a car thief named Vetz.

None of this he told to Sasha Tkach. It was only when they had driven more than thirty miles and were turning into the road that led to the house that Karpo spoke. He began the history of Yakov and Jerold and the death of Carla. Tkach nodded to show that he understood, but he looked straight ahead. Karpo pulled over to the side of the road and turned off the ignition.

"Tkach," he said, "it is essential that you understand and are attentive. The people we seek are quite dangerous."

Sasha looked out the window and then turned to face Karpo.

"I will not fail you, Emil Karpo," he said.

Karpo opened the car door and got out. So did Tkach, who checked his gun as soon as he closed the car door. They moved off the road and walked forward along the line of trees. Around a curve, about fifty yards from their car, they saw the house, a modest house before which sat a white automobile with a dented left fender scratched with the blue paint of the car it had hit after Jerold had fled with Yakov from the Kalinin Prospekt in front of the café.

The policemen moved into the cover of the trees and made their way to the side of the house so they would not be seen approaching. There was an open space of dirt and stone about fifteen yards from the trees to the house. One window faced the two men as they crossed quickly to the wall.

"Front door," Karpo said, so softly that Sasha was not sure he heard him.

Before Karpo could say another word, Tkach moved around the building to the front and strode past the parked white car to the door of the house. Karpo, who had drawn no weapon, stepped out after him as Tkach reached over to knock.

"Tkach," said Karpo, walking to join the younger man. "I did not mean for you to walk up to the door and knock."

"I'm sorry," Tkach said.

"I do not believe your suicide would have a productive result."

Tkach did not answer. He knocked at the door. Karpo moved to the side of the door and motioned Tkach out of the way. Karpo reached over and knocked. Someone stirred inside, and the door began to open. Tkach held his gun outstretched at eye level, about where the head of an average-sized man might appear.

The door was opened all the way now, and the scrawny doctor who had treated Jerold stood there calmly, paying no attention to the young man holding the gun.

"What do you want?" she said, adjusting her glasses and looking at Karpo without emotion.

"We are the police," said Karpo.

"I can see that," she said.

Tkach moved a step closer so that he could not miss.

"This automobile," said Karpo. "Is the driver here?"

"The car is mine," said the woman.

"They aren't here," said Tkach.

"We are coming in," said Karpo, and the woman backed away to let them enter.

"Why did they come here?" Tkach asked the woman impatiently. "Where are they?"

The woman moved ahead of them silently. Karpo moved into the house and said to the woman, "You have a phone?"

She nodded toward a closed door to the right of the front entrance. Karpo entered, and Sasha Tkach urged the woman into the room after him by pointing with the gun.

They were in the treatment room. It looked clean, ready. Karpo moved to the wastebasket in the corner and looked into it.

"She treated one of them for a wound," Karpo said. "Bandages, recent blood."

Karpo saw the phone on an old metal cabinet painted with white enamel and picked it up while Tkach carefully moved to the wastebasket and looked down at its bloody contents.

The woman folded her arms and waited while Karpo made his call, which began with Karpo giving someone the name of the town and the street number of the house in which they stood. It ended with Karpo saying, "*Spasee'ba*," and turning.

"Her name is Katerina Agulgan," he said. "She is a doctor. She owns an automobile, but it is not the one parked in front. Hers is a green Zil. A search for it is now being undertaken with concentration within Moscow."

"She can tell us where it is," said Sasha, moving forward to hold the gun to the right temple of the woman, who did not flinch or turn her eyes to him. Instead, she looked at Karpo, who met her gaze.

"She will not tell you, Sasha," he said.

"Then I shoot her," said Sasha, his voice breaking.

"There is nothing to be gained from her death, as there was nothing to be gained from your suicide," said Karpo.

"Something must have a resolution," said Sasha. "Something this day must conclude without confusion, without . . ." He could not find the word, but the woman did.

"Ambiguity," she said.

"She will not tell you," said Karpo, "because she is the mother of Yakov Krivonos, as the computer told us. Since the man we seek was shot, it was possible that Krivonos would bring him to his mother for treatment. Doctor, you will sit while we search your house and wait. You will sit now, in that chair."

She moved to the chair and sat.

"Sasha," he said, "you will please put your weapon away and search this house."

Tkach put his gun away, looked at the woman, and left the room, closing the door behind him.

"What is wrong with that young man?" the woman asked when Tkach had departed.

"He is brooding, Dr. Agulgan," answered Karpo. "I do not know the details, nor are they relevant to your situation."

"They are if he shoots me," she said.

"He will control himself," Karpo assured her.

"How do you know? He is a brooding Russian."

"And you are not Russian?"

She shrugged and went silent.

"Your son and the man called Jerold plan to commit

murder," Karpo said, standing erect and facing the seated woman. "You know that."

"Your partner planned to murder me a moment ago," she said.

"Yes," said Karpo.

"You want me to help a murderer find my son," she said.

"I want you to do so, but I do not expect it," said Karpo.

"What do you expect?" she asked.

"I expect nothing," he said.

The door opened, and Sasha Tkach came in holding a framed photograph in his hand.

The woman adjusted her glasses and looked at him defiantly, but she did not speak.

"Your son?" Tkach asked.

Karpo moved forward to take the photograph from Tkach, who held it at his side. Karpo looked down at the framed photograph, at the face of Yakov Krivonos as he had been perhaps ten years earlier.

The woman was sitting erect, her mouth a very thin line drawn tight. Karpo handed her the photograph, which she put gently into her lap.

"The man called Jerold will get your son killed," Karpo said.

"And if you catch him, you will kill him," she said. "I see no difference other than if I tell you where they are I betray my son."

"We will not kill your son if we can do otherwise," said Karpo.

The woman tore her eyes from the young man and looked at the ghostly figure before her. Their eyes met again, but this time there was no duel. She clutched the photograph to her chest and whispered, "I believe you."

"Do you know where they are?" he asked.

"Yes," she said. "I heard them . . . yes."

"Will you tell us?"

"Nothing is simple," she said.

"Nothing is simple," Karpo repeated, and though Tkach said nothing, he agreed.

Set well back in Soviet Square on Gorky Street stands the Central Party Archives of the Institute of Marxism-Leninism, which contains more than six thousand manuscripts of Karl Marx and Friedrich Engels and over thirty thousand documents of Lenin. Party members, politicians, and scholars who come to the building are greeted before they enter by a red granite statue of Lenin dedicated in 1938. On the outer wall of the institute is a panel with paintings of Marx, Engels, and Lenin and the bold inscription "Forward, to the Victory of Communism."

In front of Lenin, blocking his view of Gorky Street and the Moscow Soviet of Working People's Deputies, stands a four-story-high statue of Prince Yuri Dolgoruki seated triumphantly upon his horse. The prince is credited with founding Moscow more than eight hundred years ago.

The Moscow Soviet of Working People's Deputies is, as Moscow official buildings go, not terribly impressive. Built originally in 1782 as a one-story residence for the governor-general of Moscow, it was added to and rebuilt before and after the war with the Germans, complete with porticos and a balcony from which Lenin frequently addressed crowds on the street and in Soviet Square. In this building in 1917, the Revolutionary Military Council met and directed the October armed uprising in Moscow. Inside the Moscow Soviet can be found the banner of the city of Moscow. The banner bears two Orders of Lenin, the Gold Star of the Hero City, and the Order of the October Revolution.

Lenin's name is permanently on the roll of deputies of the Moscow Soviet, who, until *perestroika*, were the Communist party members responsible for running the city's services. Each of the Soviet states has its own Soviet. It is from this one in Moscow that the newly elected officials governed, and it was in Soviet Square, in front of the statue of Prince Yuri Dolgoruki, that Boris Yeltsin, the president of the Russian Soviet, and Mikhail Gorbachev, premier of the Soviet Union, would, with many other officials, generals, and party officers, be gathering in a few hours to speak at the fiftieth-anniversary celebration of the first defeat of Hitler's army in the city.

From the square in front of Prince Dolgoruki's statue, on a wooden platform that had been erected over the past two days, the speakers would be able to point to the granite in the large archways between numbers 9 and 11 on Gorky Street, granite that the Nazis had brought in from Finland to erect a victory memorial.

And Yakov Krivonos had what was undoubtedly the best seat for the coming festivities. He was seated in an almost empty room at the top of the Moscow Soviet facing Gorky Street. Access to the building had been as easy as Jerold had said it would be. Yakov had shown his photograph and identification as Yakov Shechedrin to the guard at the door, adjusted his glasses with great seriousness, and had been allowed to pass carrying his rather large briefcase. Ironically, it was Jerold who had an instant of difficulty getting in and might not have made it if the line of deputies had not been a long one behind him.

"Are you unwell, Comrade?" a uniform guard had asked a dark-suited, beard-trimmed, and quite pale Jerold.

"American flu," said Jerold.

"Yes, I'm short two men today because of it," said the guard. "My aunt says to wrap garlic around your neck and eat a clove of it twice a day."

"My mother says the same," said Jerold. "It can't hurt to try."

And with that Jerold had passed into the building. He did not join Yakov till they were on the second floor, up the stairs to the left. Even then they did not walk together. They acted as if they were busy assistants headed for bureacratic tasks in preparation for the day's events. It wasn't till they went into the stairwell door at the end of the corridor and closed the door behind them that they faced each other and spoke.

"You don't look very well, Jerold," Yakov said. "Very pale."

And, Jerold thought, you may look well, Yakov, but you are the one who is dying. May you not die too soon and may you not die too late.

"I will be fine," said Jerold, stepping past him and leading the way upward.

Yakov laughed and followed him.

"Can I take these glasses off now?" he asked.

Jerold nodded, and Yakov removed the glasses and put them in the pocket of his suit.

"I'm getting that American flu," Yakov said. "Stomach pains. Started yesterday. Worse today. I need more pills."

"When we are finished," said Jerold.

"I need more pills," Yakov said emphatically.

"When we get to the room," Jerold agreed.

They went through a door on the fourth level. It was dark, but Jerold didn't hesitate. Because of his wound, he moved slowly, but Yakov could see that he knew where he was going, around a pile of dusty stacked chairs and to a narrow door in the corner. He opened it and entered, with Yakov right behind.

They climbed again, slowly, holding the dusty handrail of the steep, narrow stairway. And then Yakov heard a door open above him, and light came down the stairway shaft. He followed Jerold up through the door and closed it.

The room was not small, about the size of the apartment from which he had thrown Carla through the window. There were ancient wooden file cabinets, six of them, lined up in one corner. Three wooden chairs sat at random places, facing nothing in particular. On the wall was a faded mural depicting factory workers marching, according to the bright lettering, to greater productivity for the Revolution. Leading the march was a woman with glasses.

"She looks like my mother," said Yakov, putting

down his briefcase on one of the chairs and opening it to reveal the parts of his rifle.

Jerold had sat in one of the other chairs. He looked back at the mural and thought the woman looked nothing like Yakov's mother, but he said, "Yes, quite a bit."

"Exactly like her," Yakov said.

"When you get the gun assembled, open the window," Jerold said.

"Pills," answered Yakov.

Timing now was everything. Jerold was greatly weakened by his wound. His loss of blood and the weakness, he knew, might be affecting his judgment, but there was no time to rest. He reached into his inner jacket pocket, removed the bottle, and took out two pills. He handed them to the waiting Yakov, who took them solemnly, gulped them down dry, and walked to the window.

"They are gathering already," he said.

"Try the window," said Jerold, putting the bottle away and enjoying the luxury of closing his eyes for an instant.

Yakov opened the window. It neither stuck nor made a sound. The window behaved perfectly, as Jerold knew it would.

"Look, Mother, top of the world," Yakov said with a chuckle.

Jerold was growing less confident of Yakov's behavior. He checked his watch. Still two hours to go. He had pills of his own to take for the pain and to keep him alert, but he would wait till he absolutely needed them, for the pills tended to cloud his judgment.

Yakov moved back to continue assembling the compact rifle.

"By day after tomorrow I'll be in Las Vegas," said Yakov as he worked.

By tomorrow, thought Jerold, you will be dead, but he said, "The day after tomorrow."

"Get a faster plane," Yakov said, holding up the assembled weapon. "The CIA can get whatever it wants."

"I've told you. I'm not with the CIA," said Jerold.

"Of course not," said Yakov. "You're just a Soviet citizen with good connections. You know what I want to do in Las Vegas?"

"Yes," said Jerold.

Yakov moved to the window.

"Don't go to the window with the gun," Jerold warned. "Not yet."

"No," said Yakov. "I don't mean the girls with the feathers. I want them, yes. The girls with the feathers. But I want to go to the top of that big hotel-casino in the pictures. I want to stand on top of it and look down at the lights in the night. I want to spread my arms and have them turn into wings so I can leap over the edge. Maybe I can do it with one of those hang gliders."

"Maybe," said Jerold.

"And I will meet Madonna," he said seriously, turning to the seated Jerold.

"You will meet Madonna," said Jerold.

"And she will be very grateful for what I have done," he said.

"Very grateful," said Jerold.

"You think I'm a fool, don't you?" asked Yakov.

"I know you are not a fool," said Jerold. "You would not have been chosen for this assignment if you were a fool."

"Your Lee Harvey Oswald was not a fool, either," said Yakov. "Will I be as famous in America as he is in the Soviet Union?"

"Yes," said Jerold, feeling quite weak but trying not to show it.

Yakov moved back to the window and looked down.

"Top of the world," he said.

TWELVE

Considering his rank and the visibility of his public office, the Gray Wolfhound lived in a very modest two-story house off the Outer Ring Road, twenty minutes by car and driver from his office in Petrovka. It would have taken little more than a word or a hint to have someone ousted from a large apartment in the city, but the Wolfhound wanted none of it.

Colonel Snitkonoy enjoyed entertaining visiting dignitaries in his home, liked to show the almost Spartan nature of his existence to foreigners. The colonel harbored a dream, which he shared on occasion with the two members of his household, a dream of this modest house being turned into a small birthplace museum.

The two members of the colonel's household with whom this dream was shared were his retired adjutant, a quiet, devoted, and very stupid man named Golovin, who firmly believed that the colonel was the most brilliant military officer in the long history of all the Russias, and a housekeeper, Lena, who was not in the least bit stupid and was quite sure that when the colonel moved or died the house would be leveled and replaced with a massive apartment building or offices.

Each morning, seven days each week, except when he had an early-morning engagement or had to catch a flight out of Moscow, a car and driver would be parked and waiting at five-thirty in front of the modest house. The car that waited was also modest, a Zhiguli of recent vintage, not one of the large Volgas or even a foreign car, which he could afford and to which both Golovin and Lena said he was entitled.

This morning, Colonel Snitkonoy was slightly annoyed. He would be attending the ceremony in Soviet Square, and it was especially important that his dress uniform be spotless, his ribbons even, his hat without crease or blemish. He had drunk his morning coffee with care, eaten his English toast with caution, finished his glass of Turkish orange juice with dignity, and discovered a speck of something oily on his knee with concealed horror.

This speck had forced the Wolfhound to completely change his uniform and to be ten minutes late going through the front door, where Golovin on cloudy mornings like this stood ready with an umbrella to walk with the colonel to the waiting car, should the threatening rain start.

But this proved to be a morning like no other morning. Golovin stood inside the door with the umbrella, but he did not open either door or umbrella. Instead, he said, "You have a visitor."

The Wolfhound stopped, waited.

"He said it was urgent. Inspector Rostnikov. I put

him in your office. I asked him not to touch anything.
I hope that was acceptable. He said—"

"Tell the driver I will be out shortly," said the Wolfhound, going to a door just off of the entranceway.
When Golovin was out the front door, the colonel
entered his office.

Rostnikov was seated in the large wooden chair across
from the desk. His leg, the one he had injured as a boy
in the war, was propped up on a wooden block the
colonel kept before the chair as a footrest. The block
had a history that the colonel enjoyed relating to his
guests, but this was neither the time nor the guest.
Rostnikov wore a jacket and no tie. He needed a shave
and looked quite tired.

"Would you like a coffee, Porfiry Petrovich?" asked
the colonel.

"That would be pleasant," said Rostnikov, and the
colonel moved to the door, where he ordered the now-
waiting Golovin to bring coffee.

The colonel turned back into the room in anticipa-
tion. Rostnikov had never come to his house before. He
had never been invited to his house. Even when Rostnikov had brought him the information that resulted in
the dismissal of a high-ranking KGB officer just a few
months ago, the information and evidence had been
brought to the colonel's office.

That information had resulted in Colonel Snitkonoy's
being taken far more seriously than he had been before,
which was both a good and a bad thing.

"You are supposed to be on vacation in Yalta, Inspector," the Gray Wolfhound said, moving to his desk. He

leaned against the desk and folded his arms in front of him.

"Why was I sent on vacation, Colonel?"

Rostnikov asked the question gently, casually, and he would have liked to present it more carefully, in the natural context of a conversation, but there was no time.

"An order came to all departments indicating those senior officers who were overdue for vacation and who must take them immediately," said the colonel.

"And would you remember the names on the list?" asked Rostnikov. "I mean, remember them if you saw them."

"Yes," said the colonel. "I would remember all of those within the MVD and— Where is this leading, Inspector? I have an important ceremony to attend."

Rostnikov shifted his weight, reached into his pocket, came up with Vasilievich's notebook, and handed it to the Wolfhound as Golovin knocked at the door.

"Come in," called the colonel, looking down at the book. "Put it on the desk."

Golovin looked concerned but said nothing as he put down the tray containing two cups and a steaming pot. Golovin departed quickly, closing the door behind him.

"Page six," said Rostnikov. "May I help myself?"

"Please," said the Wolfhound, turning the pages of the notebook while Rostnikov reached over to pour himself coffee.

"These are the names, not all of them, but many of them," he said, looking away from the book at Rostnikov.

"Now look at pages nine through twelve," Rostnikov said, lifting the cup to his lips.

"Where did you get this notebook?"

"It belonged to a GRU inspector named Vasilievich. He was murdered in Yalta two days ago. The men who murdered him were hired by an American who was himself hired by a Soviet. The American returned to the United States yesterday before he could be properly detained."

"I see," said the colonel wisely, though he saw nothing at all, and then on the tenth page he saw more names, names that he recognized, including that of both Gorbachev and Yeltsin, but the one that caught the colonel's eye immediately was his own name. He looked away from the notebook again at Rostnikov, who put his coffee cup down on the tray.

"Vasilievich was convinced that a conspiracy existed, a conspiracy engineered among high-ranking officers in the police and intelligence services," said Rostnikov. "The conspiracy required removing from Moscow and other key cities the senior investigators who might possibly uncover the conspiracy."

"Assassination," said the colonel, tapping the book against his thigh.

"That is what Vasilievich believed."

"And what you believe?"

"Yes," said Rostnikov.

"I am on this list," said the colonel.

Rostnikov said nothing.

The colonel nodded his head knowingly, placed the notebook down carefully, and reached for one of the cups of coffee. Conflicting feelings surged through the Wolfhound, not the least of which was a certain pride at being considered important enough to be included on the list of people who might be worth assassinating. Fear was not one of the feelings, for, in truth, Colonel Snitkonoy was a very brave man.

"What do you propose, Inspector?"

"I have reason to believe that the assassination in Moscow is to be carried out by a young man named Yakov Krivonos, the man I was in the process of locating when I was sent on vacation."

"And the man Inspector Karpo continued to search for until I ordered him on vacation," continued the colonel. "A vacation ordered by directive."

"Inspectors Karpo and Tkach are in pursuit of Krivonos and a man named Jerold, who may be behind the planned attempt," said Rostnikov. "May I have more coffee?"

"Help yourself," said the colonel.

"Inspector Karpo has until tonight at midnight, according to your order, before he must go on vacation," said Rostnikov.

"If we can reach Inspector Karpo, inform him that the order is no longer in effect," said the colonel. "You have a suggestion, Inspector?"

"One that may be dangerous, Colonel."

"Proceed."

"A call from you to the appropriate heads of departments in the KGB, MVD, and GRU indicating that you have evidence of such an assassination plot and advising them to be alert. You might also tell them about the notebook and suggest that copies have been made and are safe."

"One or more of the people I contact may well be part of the conspiracy, Porfiry Petrovich."

"Let us hope so, Colonel. Let us hope they realize that they must stop the assassination attempts or risk exposure. If nothing happens, then Vasilievich's notebook is the conjecture of an old man who coincidentally was murdered. If even one assassination takes place, the conspirators will be pursued. They had hoped, perhaps, to make it look like the work of a group of young drug dealers and criminals acting from a grievance against the state. We must disabuse them of the possibility of such a public interpretation."

"I will make the calls immediately. I can also attempt to have the celebration in Soviet Square postponed."

"There is less than an hour," said Rostnikov, rising from his chair. "Will they listen?"

"No," said the Wolfhound. "They will not. And if I am not on the stand with the other officials and an assassination attempt does take place, I will be an immediate suspect. I must make these calls quickly, Inspector, and I must do them in plenty of time to get to Soviet Square."

It was not the first time that Rostnikov had felt a sincere admiration for the colonel, and he hoped it would not be the last.

"We must hope that Inspectors Karpo and Tkach locate the assassin," the Wolfhound said, reaching for the phone.

As he leaned forward, his leg brushed his waiting cup of coffee. A splash of dark brown hit his immaculately clean trousers. The colonel paid no attention.

* * *

Gorky Street was cordoned off for the celebration. Even if Karpo and Tkach had identified themselves as policemen, they could have gotten no closer because of the crowds. Karpo pulled to the curb in front of the Moscow News Office and across from Puskhin Square. They got out and battled through the crowds onto Gorky Street, making their way past the All-Russia Theatrical Society, the Nikolai Ostrovsky Museum, and Food Store Number One. In front of the Tsentralnaya Hotel they crossed the street to the sidewalk before the Druzhba Bookshop.

Yakov's mother had told them where to find her son, and Karpo had considered several possibilities. One possibility was to call Petrovka, to tell the duty officer to get to the Moscow Soviet, but there would be a great risk in that. That there was a conspiracy was evident from even his cryptic conversations with Inspector Rostnikov over the last two days. There was no telling who would receive his call or how it might be treated.

No, there had been ample time for him and Tkach to get to Gorky Street, and though it had taken longer than they anticipated, they were here now, making their way through the crowds. Tkach was markedly improved but not to be fully trusted. Had he an alternative, Karpo would have sent Tkach back to Petrovka, but there was no time for alternatives.

Tkach looked across the broad street at the raised platform on which minor officials were already gathering in spite of the thunder and almost certain rain. The threat of rain had not deterred the crowd, which hoped the occasion would be one of protests and spectacle.

Karpo led the way into the building and to the guards.

"Two men," he said, showing his identification card, though both of the guards had recognized him. "One young, wearing glasses, the other about my age, bearded, probably quite pale."

The guard had no idea what Karpo's age might be, but he shook his head and said, "Hundreds of people have come in and out this morning, all of them with proper identification."

The second guard, however, said, "The one with the flu."

"Yes, perhaps," said the first guard. "He had a beard, but—"

"Where is he?" asked Karpo.

Both guards shrugged.

"I think," said the second guard, "he went up those steps."

Karpo and Tkach hurried past the guards and moved up the stairs two or three at a time.

It took them almost a minute to make their way to the fourth floor, past officials in the halls hurrying for raincoats and umbrellas in their offices or scurrying down the stairs to be outside, where they could be seen when the celebration speeches began. It took them another few minutes to find the door on the fourth floor with the stairway behind it. They entered and in the darkness moved up slowly, cautiously, Karpo in the lead, weapons drawn.

When he reached the door, Karpo stopped and

reached back to halt Tkach. Then slowly, ever so slowly, he began to turn the handle, hoping that the growing crowd on the street and the sound of voices inside the room would cover whatever noise he might make. Before he could push the door open, two shots screamed like wounded jackals inside the room.

The rain had begun almost as soon as Karpo and Tkach had entered the Moscow Soviet building. The rain had started to fall, and the umbrellas had begun to open on the street as the major officials began arriving with their own umbrellas. The platform was not covered. No one had anticipated the weather. It should not have rained today. But it was raining, and Yakov Krivonos was propped at his window, ready to fire.

The problem was "Almost all of them on the platform are wearing raincoats, and some of them have umbrellas. I can't see most of their faces. How am I supposed to know who to shoot?"

Jerold forced himself out of the chair and moved to the window. "The first three on the left, near the flag, see them?"

"Yes."

"You will shoot them. And two over. The one with the boots. See him? The one who just climbed up?"

"I see his boots," said Yakov.

"Shoot him, too," said Jerold, wearily moving back to the chair.

"Hell with this," Yakov decided as he moved the rifle to the window, lay on the ground, and propped the weapon up on the inverted metal V that served as a

bipod to steady the already steady weapon. "The longer
we wait, the harder the rain will be and the more
the targets will protect themselves and be harder to
find."

Yakov Krivonos nestled the butt of the rifle against
his shoulder, pressed his face against the cheek rest,
and moved his left hand to the pistol grip and his right
hand to the wooden piece in front of the trigger. The
weapon was compact, the barrel clamped at the front
and rear to ensure the torque initiated by a bullet passing through the bore would not lift the barrel away
from the intended point of aim. The barrel was as long
as that on almost any sniper weapon, but it ran the
full length of the rifle, almost to the end of the short,
comfortable butt. The Walther RA 2000 was gas operated, easy to handle, with the ejection port close to the
person firing. Thus, there were both right-handed and
left-handed versions so that the port would be on the
side opposite the sniper. It was accurate within three
inches at a thousand yards.

"What are you thinking, Yakov?" Jerold asked, his
voice dropping, near exhaustion.

Yakov's solution was simple. He would shoot everyone on the platform. There were twelve men and two
women. Jerold hadn't told him whom not to shoot. He
had simply identified those who were to die. A few
extras wouldn't matter, and Yakov didn't want the
American to try to get out of his promises of wealth
and women. He raised his rifle. He would simply shoot
them all.

"Yakov, you will shoot only those . . ."

Yakov heard him but did not wish to, and so he told

himself a lie. He told himself he had begun to fire before Jerold spoke. He fired the first shot, and the second came almost immediately after.

Before the echo of the second shot had wept its last tear of pain through the stairwell, Karpo pushed the door open and stepped into the room, gun level, ready to fire. He knew where the window would be, must be. If both of the men they sought were in the room, he would go for the one near the window, the one who must be preparing to shoot down another Soviet official in the square.

Karpo came very close to squeezing the trigger before he realized that the person leaning forward against the window with a rifle in his hands was half-turned and looking straight up at the ceiling, blood streaming out of his mouth. As Tkach scrambled up the stairs and joined him, Karpo swung around to the far corner and found Jerold, his hands raised high over his head.

"My gun is on the floor, over there," said Jerold, nodding with his head toward the weapon, about five feet in front of him on the floor.

"Sasha," Karpo said, and Tkach leveled his gun at Jerold while Karpo moved to the window to look down. There seemed to be confusion on the platform, and people were looking up at him through the rain, but he could see people scrambling in confusion. One person had fallen.

"He was about to shoot President Gorbachev," said Jerold. "May I put my hands down? I'm feeling quite weak."

"No," said Sasha, and Jerold could see that as much as his arms ached and his knees threatened to quit beneath him, it would be best to remain exactly as he was.

Karpo quickly examined the dead Yakov Krivonos and turned to Jerold.

"My pocket," Jerold said. "Rear. Take out my wallet. I'm a KGB officer."

Karpo moved toward him quickly. The room would soon be filled with armed soldiers from the street, soldiers who would have to be stopped before they entered the room and began firing.

"Sasha," Karpo said. "Go down the stairs. Tell them who you are, that everything is all right."

Tkach put his gun away, looking at the dead young man near the window, and felt a sudden chill through the open window as he moved through the door.

"My name is Alexandrov," said Jerold, his American accent suddenly gone. "I was trying to locate and identify all of the members of an extended extortion and drug gang. Yakov was my link. He thought I was an American drug dealer."

Karpo turned the pale man around and removed the wallet from his back pocket. He found the secret compartment and removed the KGB identity card with Jerold's photograph.

"It is authentic," said Jerold.

Below them they could both hear boots hurrying upward through the building.

"I am sure it is," said Karpo.

"You almost killed me this morning, Inspector

Karpo," he said, putting his hands down and sinking into the chair.

"And you almost killed me," said Karpo.

"Had to make it look good for Yakov. I am sorry."

Karpo nodded.

"You understand?" Jerold went on as they heard Tkach's voice below, though his words were unclear.

"Not completely," said Karpo.

"But you believe me?" said Jerold, looking up, his shirt drenched with sweat.

"No," said Karpo.

"It would be best for you to believe me, Inspector Karpo," Jerold said. "I'm about to make us heroes."

With that, a major, his brown uniform dark and heavy with rain, his cap pulled down, came rushing into the room. His gun was drawn but at his side, indicating that Sasha had been reasonably convincing.

"Major," Jerold said, "I am Lieutenant Vasili Alexandrov, KGB Security Division. The man at the window is Yakov Krivonos. He was about to kill President Gorbachev. Inspector Karpo arrived just as I prevented him from doing so."

The major looked at the two men, trying to decide which one was more pale. The scene was unnatural, a moment frozen from some half-remembered play, and the major, who had witnessed many deaths in Afghanistan, felt a cold chill and knew this moment would haunt him till he died.

THIRTEEN

The next morning, the sun shone on Moscow.

Shortly before nine, under that shining sun, tourists from both within the Soviet Union and beyond its formerly formidable borders boarded the excursion boats at the Kiev pier. There weren't many sightseers this early in the morning. Among those boarding, however, though not together, were a tall, quite pale man whom everyone avoided as best they could and a block of a man with a limp who was ignored by the people scrambling ahead of him to get the best seats.

Porfiry Petrovich did not want the best seat, and Emil Karpo did not care. Before the ship had pulled away from the pier, Rostnikov was seated along the port rail in a chair with its view partly obstructed by a thick metal pole. Almost all the other passengers were in front of the ship with their guidebooks out. Rostnikov was very much alone when Karpo joined him as they pulled away from the pier and the ship began its journey.

"Have you ever taken this ride before, Emil Karpo?"

"I have not."

"Over there," said Rostnikov, pointing to the bank. "The fortress walls of the old Novo-Devichy Convent. See the belfry?"

"I see it," said Karpo.

"In the convent cathedral, Boris Godunov was proclaimed czar in 1597," said Rostnikov.

"It was 1598," Karpo corrected.

Rostnikov smiled.

"You knew that," said Karpo, looking at him.

"Perhaps," said Rostnikov, still looking at the bank. "The wife and sister of Peter the Great were imprisoned in the convent for plotting against Peter. Many famous people are buried inside those walls. I know you know this, Emil Karpo, but it gives me some small pleasure to say it aloud, so please indulge me while we wait. Sarah and I made this trip with Iosef when he was a boy."

Karpo looked at his colleague and saw a weariness he had never seen before.

"You are ill," he said.

"I am tired," Porfiry Petrovich corrected.

"What is it that we are waiting for?" asked Karpo.

"An answer," said Rostnikov.

The ship passed the sports complex of Luzhniki, and over the cabin of the boat Karpo could see the Lenin Hills coming down to the edge of the water and, high on top, against the skyline, the massive main building of Moscow University, its tower lost for the moment in a low cloud.

"Beautiful," said Rostnikov with a sigh.

Karpo said nothing as they went under the double-level bridge.

"Yes," said Karpo, though the mystery of beauty had either eluded him or, as he thought more likely, existed only as a bourgeois fantasy.

Karpo was aware of the man approaching them well before he turned to face him. The man was in his mid-forties, thin, balding, and dark, dressed in a blue suit with a matching striped tie.

"Colonel Zhenya," Rostnikov said, looking up and shielding his eyes against the sun with his hand in what might have been taken for a mock salute.

The KGB colonel was known to both Karpo and Rostnikov. He stood erect and played with a ring on his right hand as he spoke.

"I do not believe I have ever seen you out of uniform before," Rostnikov said.

Zhenya looked at Karpo and then at Rostnikov without moving his head.

"My presence doesn't surprise you, does it, Rostnikov?" he said.

"I am completely surprised," said Rostnikov with what might well be taken for surprise.

"You are tired from your flight, and you have not slept for almost two days," said Zhenya. "That, I assume, is why you are engaging in pallid irony."

"You are certainly right, Colonel," Rostnikov said, shifting his leg as he remembered why it was that he had not taken this river ride or any other for many years. The dampness cramped his leg in wet, relentless fingers.

"You were well aware that your conversations were monitored and that someone listening, someone who knew your background, would probably understand your little code," said Zhenya.

"I was counting on it, Colonel," said Rostnikov.

"There, see, you are right. I should never say anything like that to a KGB colonel, especially to you."

"At least," said Zhenya, "you would not have done so before the dismantling of the Soviet Union, which is now under way."

"I should not do so now," said Rostnikov. "But I am tired."

Emil Karpo stood silently, listening.

Zhenya looked at him and said, "Congratulations, Inspector Karpo," he said. "I understand you are a hero. You participated in thwarting the assassination of our president. Only a minor official of no consequence was wounded."

There was no irony to be detected in the colonel's words.

"Thank you," said Karpo.

"And you, Rostnikov, you are a hero, too, a silent hero, a hero behind the scenes," Zhenya said, suddenly abandoning the ring he had been playing with and moving to the rail. "You prevented a conspiracy to end the leaders of the reform. You should be very proud of yourself."

"I simply forwarded information to my superior," said Rostnikov, deciding to suffer the cramping agony in his leg rather than stand and show Colonel Zhenya that he was nervous or, worse, rising to challenge him.

Zhenya leaned on the rail. Beyond him, on the shore,

Rostnikov could see the diving boards of the Moskva Swimming Pool. A man on the top board leaped off gracelessly. Zhenya turned and looked back at the two men.

"I see a question in your eyes, Rostnikov," he said. "Do you wish to ask it?"

Rostnikov said nothing, and Emil Karpo stood motionless.

"You want to know why I am here. You expected me, but you did not know why I would come. You were disturbed by what has happened, but you did not know quite what to conclude. I will enlighten you, Rostnikov. I will enlighten you because you have once again been used. I will enlighten you because I want you to know that you have been used."

"I appreciate that you would not be here if you did not intend to enlighten me," said Rostnikov.

"I did not order Georgi Vasilievich murdered," Zhenya said. "If I had, I would tell you now, for there is nothing you could do about it. That murder was ordered by the man who organized the conspiracy, which you and Karpo thwarted with the help of one of my men."

"Misha Ivanov is one of your men," said Rostnikov.

"Yes," said Zhenya. "The notebook that you brought to Colonel Snitkonoy was a fake. Misha Ivanov planted it for you to find. Vasilievich's notebook, which was full of nonsense and would have led you in the wrong direction, was destroyed. You are wondering two things at this moment. First, given my own lack of sympathy for the current reforms, why did I not let the conspiracy take place and simply benefit from it? Second, if I did not want the conspiracy to take place, why did I not simply reveal it myself and take credit? I need not hide from you that I have ambitions, that I wish to serve the Revolution and not participate in its destruction. Have you figured out where we are going with this yet, Inspector?"

Rostnikov could stand it no longer. He raised himself from the chair and leaned forward with both hands on the horizontal pipe before him to keep from falling. Rostnikov had figured it out, but it might well be essential to his survival to allow Colonel Zhenya to outwit him. Rostnikov resisted the urge to look at Karpo.

"I am in your hands, Colonel," Porfiry Petrovich said.

"The conspiracy the two of you helped to thwart was not aimed at Gorbachev and the reformers," said Zhenya. "It was aimed at the true patriots, the old guard and those of us who support the Revolution. It was not the Stalinists who planned to kill but the reformers who plotted to end opposition, to kill the Stalinists. Rostnikov, I was certainly one of the intended victims. The idea was to blame the entire operation on the CIA, Americans who wanted to keep Gorbachev in power. I needed honest policemen like you to step in. It is quite possible that you have now earned the enmity of the very people you thought you were saving from death. Now that is irony, Porfiry Petrovich Rostnikov. As a Russian, you should appreciate that. Now you may smile. Karpo, you have a question."

"Alexandrov," Karpo said so quietly that the word was almost obscured by the purring engine of the ship.

"Jerold," corrected Zhenya. "He was part of the con-

spiracy. He had several options. If Krivonos had succeeded, Alexandrov would have escaped and left him to
his fate, assuming that Krivonos, if he survived, would
identify an American as the man who had hired him to
do the deed. If Krivonos failed, as he did, Alexandrov
would kill him, as he did, and emerge a hero. See how
honest I am being with the two of you?"

Rostnikov allowed himself a glance at Karpo, whose
attention was riveted on the colonel.

"You have helped our cause, the true cause of the
Revolution, to survive to do battle another day," said
Zhenya. "Inspector Karpo, you, as a zealous and loyal
member of the party, might, I would think, be content
with this outcome that holds open hope of maintaining
the old order."

"Within the old society the elements of a new one
have been created," said Karpo. "The dissolution of the
old ideas keeps even pace with the dissolution of the
old conditions of existence."

Zhenya shook his head.

"You are becoming a reformer, one of *them*, Inspector
Karpo," he said.

"Those were not my words, Colonel," said Karpo.
"They were written by Karl Marx and Friedrich Engels. They are part of the *Communist Manifesto*."

Colonel Zhenya looked first at the man known as the
Washtub, who was trying to hide his pain, and then
at the cadaverous creature who stood beside him and
wondered how such naïveté could survive. It had been
foolish to seek them out, to savor his victory. It had
been self-indulgent, a mistake he would never make

again. Without another word, Colonel Zhenya walked to the front of the boat and lost himself in the crowd.

"Well, Emil Karpo. What do you think?"

"I do not think, Inspector Rostnikov. I enforce the law."

"And I, Emil Karpo, think too much. We are cursed by a disease of opposites. It may account for our compatibility."

"I was not aware that you considered us to be compatible," said Karpo as Rostnikov moved slightly to his right, urging feeling and circulation back into his leg. He checked his watch. There was still an hour to go on the ride.

FOURTEEN

On a spring evening, a very few months ago, three policemen, two in Moscow and one in Livadia, less than two miles from Yalta, were out walking at the same precise moment.

Before the night was over, one of the men would be laughing, one would be crying, and the third would be showing no emotion whatsoever.

This was not, Emil Karpo was sure, the ultimate solution to his increasingly frequent moments of uncertainty. He walked because he did not wish to be close to people on the Metro or a bus. He did not wish to be reminded of his own existence, did not wish to hear people talk of what had happened the day before. He walked knowing that when he reached his destination he would have respite from the memory of Colonel Zhenya.

Karpo had become a policeman because it was at once the easiest and most difficult thing he could do. It was easy because he felt confident that the law was, basically, simple and direct, and the philosophy behind it was evident. Crime was crime. The goal of the Soviet state was the total success of the Revolution. That which prevented the success of the Revolution was politically wrong. Murder, rape, robbery, fraud, corruption, those were easy, those were clearly counterrevolutionary. Crime was a rejection of the goals of the state, roadblocks, setbacks. He looked at himself, as Porfiry Petrovich had once said, as a determined tractor whose function was to remove an endless line of fallen logs along the road of the tank of Revolution.

It was the responsibility of the leaders of the party to set the policy of the Revolution in light of internal and external events. But now the party was not in command; the law was being interpreted by suntanned men who wished to be exactly like those against whom they had for so long struggled. What was the meaning of their life? What was the meaning of the life of Emil Karpo? It had never been a question before, but it had come to him increasingly in the past months.

He was gradually coming to the conclusion that had always been evident to many of those around him. One's loyalty should be given to those whom one trusts, and to them only, not to an abstraction called the State.

This was a new concept for Karpo.

He could neither embrace the return to the past represented by Zhenya nor give his allegiance to the new leaders who had abandoned the Revolution and were now behaving like Americans or the French to keep and consolidate their power.

It was at that moment that Emil Karpo, as he opened

the door to the apartment building, first seriously considered the possibility of resigning his position as a police officer.

He knocked at the door to the apartment, though he knew the door would be open, that the aunt and cousin would be out. Mathilde answered the door. The amused smile was on her face; her dark brown hair hung loosely around her shoulders. She had on no makeup, and she wore a plain blue dress. She could have been a housewife in the midst of cleaning house.

Their relationship had grown more complex than he had ever anticipated. In truth, Emil Karpo had anticipated no relationship other than one that provided him respite from the animal necessity that he could not deny. But something more had happened. She had become—for reasons that Karpo could not identify and that might not exist, since Mathilde did not function on the basis of reason—his friend. Mathilde Verson and Porfiry Petrovich Rostnikov were the only people he had known since he was a boy, and that included his own parents, who seemed to display any concern for him.

"Emil Karpo, for a hero of the Revolution who has saved the life of the president himself, you look even more serious than usual, and the usual is about as serious as a human being can get."

With this she stepped back and let him enter. She closed the door behind him and stood as he turned to her.

"The tea is warm, and we can talk about life and the state before we go to bed," she said, moving past him to the curtain that separated the small living room from the kitchen area. Beyond the kitchen was the single bedroom with the oversized prerevolutionary bed.

"I do not wish to talk," said Karpo, following Mathilde as she moved to the pot boiling gently on the stove.

"Then let's just drink our tea and—"

"I do not wish to drink tea," he said.

She turned to him, put her hands on her hips, and tilted her head to one side. The puzzled smile disappeared from her face as Karpo moved toward her and reached out to touch her left breast.

"Emil Karpo, with what drug has someone secretly injected you?"

Karpo gripped her arms firmly but gently, and she looked up into his pale face. Something very like tears were forming in his eyes, and she did not know whether to be frightened or very pleased.

Sasha Tkach, closely shaven, walked into the hospital in clean clothes. His hair was combed back, and Maya had put a touch of hair tonic on it to keep it from falling forward into his face. Under his left arm he held a package wrapped in green paper.

No one stopped him as he went to the elevator and informed the thin woman who operated it that he wanted the sixth floor. He was the only passenger, but she stopped at each floor along the way. He was not disturbed. No one got on.

"Thank you," he said, getting out when the doors finally opened on six.

The nurses on duty at the station did not ask Sasha Tkach for identification or where he was going. He moved down the hall and into the ward where Zelach had been moved following his recovery from surgery.

Other patients in the eight-bed ward had visitors; some had two or three, and one man in the corner seemed to be having a party. Zelach was lying back, his face almost as white as Karpo's, his left eye covered by a bandage, his right eye closed. Sasha moved to the side of the bed and quietly said, "Arkady."

There was no answer. Sasha put the package down, found a folding chair in the corner of the room against the wall, returned to the bedside with it open, and sat. Five minutes later, when Zelach stirred to the sound of laughter from the party in the corner, Tkach repeated, "Arkady."

And Zelach opened his eye. The lid fluttered, and Zelach seemed to be having trouble focusing. He turned his head slowly and found Sasha. Zelach's swollen lips formed something that might have been a smile.

"Sasha," he said dryly.

"Would you like a drink, some water?" asked Tkach, geting up from the chair.

"No," Zelach said in a dry voice that was not his own. "Have you forgiven me?"

"Arkady, it is you who should forgive me."

"Me?"

"Yes."

"I forgive you, Sasha, but I don't—"

"Your mother says your eye will be saved. You will need glasses. You'll look like an intellectual."

"I'll look," Zelach rasped, "like a potato sack with glasses."

"You are too hard on yourself, Arkady."

"No, I am not, Sasha Tkach. It is you who is too hard on himself. You are only a human being. See, I can think of nothing to say but my mother's old sayings."

"You are right, Arkady Zelach," said Tkach.

"My mother said you and Karpo are heroes," said Zelach, trying to raise his head. "Or was I dreaming?"

"We were not heroes."

Zelach held back the sharp pain in his face as he propped himself higher and turned his head far enough toward Tkach that he could see the green paper of the package lying on the small table near his bed.

"What is that?"

"Open it," said Tkach.

"I don't think—"

"I'll open it for you," Tkach said, taking the package and carefully opening it so that Zelach could give the wrapping paper to his mother if he wished to do so. The contents of the package were small, a packet of papers about the size of an eyeglass case.

"Shall I read it?" Tkach said.

"Yes," Zelach said as a peal of laughter came from the party in the corner and a patient somewhere in the ward began coughing uncontrollably.

Sasha Tkach read:

" 'Upon recovery from injuries received in the course of his duties, Arkady Sergeivich Zelach will take two weeks of vacation in the Crimean region of the Ukrainian Republic at the Lermontov Hotel in Yalta. There will be no expenses incurred for this period, and

Arkady Sergeivich Zelach will be permitted to be accompanied by his wife or any immediate member of his family.' "

"My mother," said Zelach.

"Arkady, my wife and I will be going with you. I have also been given a vacation. My wife's family is in Nikopol. We will see them for several days and then join you and your mother, if that pleases you."

"You want to go on a vacation with me and my mother?" asked Arkady incredulously.

"Very much," said Sasha Tkach.

"Does that mean we are friends?" Zelach asked.

"I would consider it an honor," said Tkach with a laugh.

At the airport in Yalta, Porfiry Petrovich Rostnikov was met by his wife, who handed him an envelope that had been delivered to the hotel just before Sarah had left for the airport.

Rostnikov's leg had already been aching from the boat ride that morning, but the cramped conditions on the plane and the turbulent weather that made it impossible to get up and walk about had led Rostnikov to consider seeking medical help. He had tried sleeping on the plane. Impossible. He had managed to finish the book he had begun on the flight to Moscow, an Ed McBain tale, *Let's Hear It for the Deaf Man*. He had read the book many times before. The pages were now, like many of his favorite books in his American detective-novel collection, unglued and ready to escape from the battered cover that held them loosely together. It helped a bit, but he could not read for more than a few minutes at a time.

He took the envelope and looked at his wife in the red-sun twilight. Her hair had grown back quickly since the surgery, and though he knew there was a scar, it could not be seen. She had lost weight, but she was still a solid woman whose face was remarkably unlined considering the roughness of the life she had led for her forty-eight years.

"Porfiry Petrovich," his wife said, looking over the top of her glasses as she had done since the day he had first met her. "You are ill."

"And you are quite beautiful," he said.

"That is your fever talking."

"No," he said, opening the envelope. There was a single-spaced typed, unsigned sheet inside. He read it, put it back in the envelope, and put the envelope into his pocket.

"What is wrong, Porfiry?"

"Nothing. My leg, that's all. And I need sleep."

"Can you sleep with this pain?"

People were moving past them, around them.

"We shall see," he said.

"We shall not see, Porfiry Petrovich. We shall find a physician and get you something for your pain. Then you will go to bed, and I will bring you soup and medicine and take care of you."

"You are not well enough yet," Rostnikov said, stopping to regain his strength.

He looked at her in the evening light, and she shook her head.

"I'm well enough, Porfiry Petrovich. I've been lying

around recovering for weeks. I'd like to feel useful. Will you deprive me of the opportunity to feel useful for the first time in months?"

"I will not," he said, moving again but trying to put as little weight on his wife as he possibly could.

"Enjoy being ill," she said. "You deserve it. Porfiry Petrovich, I have never asked you a question about your work. Is this true?"

"Yes," he said as they entered the bright airport terminal.

"What is in the envelope?"

"A KGB colonel named Zhenya has met with an accident," he said. "He fell over the side of one of the tourist boats on the Moscow River and was pulled into the propeller."

"And you knew this man?"

"I knew this man," said Rostnikov, wondering how many other officers in the MVD, KGB, and GRU would be having accidents in the near future.

"It's time you stopped thinking for a while," Sarah said, letting go of her husband's arm so he could make his own way with dignity through the crowded waiting room of the airport. "If you cannot stop thinking on your vacation, when can you?"

"Yes," Rostnikov agreed, taking a step on his own, "when can you?"